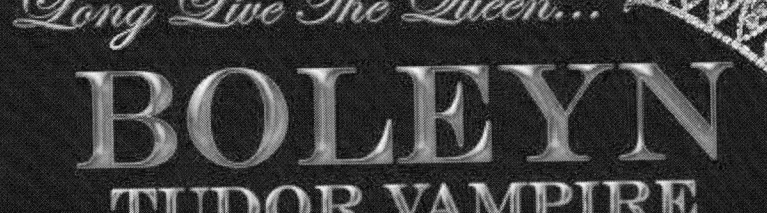

Long Live The Queen...
BOLEYN
TUDOR VAMPIRE

Cinsearae S.

BOLEYN--Tudor Vampire
©2010 by Cinsearae S.
Cover Design by C.R. Santiago

All rights reserved.

This is a work of fiction. Names, characters, places, dialogue and incidents are either the product of the author's imagination or are used fictitiously. Any resemblance to actual persons, living or dead, business establishments, events or locales is entirely coincidental.

No part of this book may be used or reproduced in any form without permission from the author, except by a reviewer, who may quote brief passages in articles or reviews.

http://BloodTouch.Webs.Com Official Author Website

ISBN: 1451559496
EAN-13: 9781451559491

1st printing

Printed in the United States of America

BOLEYN
Tudor Vampire

Cinsearae S.

Chapter One

I lived in a time when wars were commonplace. Wars often born out of religious revolts, a lust for power over others, or, my personal favorite: *fear*. Fear of *losing* that power -- that control one had over his people and the lands he ruled over.

Much blood was spilt in my day, the grounds soaked with that of the innocent -- women, children, the elderly -- none were safe from the tyranny of a mad, corrupted king who demanded his people recognize him as the one true sovereign... just as high as God himself. Those who recognized none other but Our Almighty as their savior were put to death.

A man that has been given too much power surely loses his mind, indeed. Perhaps it is partially my fault, as I helped him to discover such hidden powers that eventually made him untouchable in the eyes of parliament, and The Pope himself.

I mingled with deceivers, as I was a deceiver myself. I knew my deception would come back to haunt me, and I knew there was no escaping it. The lies, the treachery, even adultery was oh, so trite and routine. Promises meant nothing. They were but mere empty words. And the promises of a king just as fallible and worthless.

He was remembered not only for his 'greatness', but for his insanity as well. I too, fell prey to his bouts of madness. In love one moment, out of love the next. No one was safe from his wanderlust. Any woman who valued and cherished their chastity was wise to stay away from court, else they would fall prey to his wiles.

I was no match for my own wild and jealous heart. Any woman whom I found wenching with the king or merely saw favor in his eyes, I had either removed from court, or beheaded. It was hard keeping the more bloodthirsty actions from my husband. He greatly disapproved of me getting too close to his private affairs, and over time, I fell more and more out of favor with the king.

And although I too, was drunk on power and prestige, I was always filled with a cold dread, some strange knowledge that weighed heavily on my soul. I was like a bird in a gilded cage, my wings clipped for added measure. The king wanted a male heir to the throne. He already had two daughters -- one from his former queen, Katharine, and myself -- but I had yet to produce a son. For all that I knew what would happen to me later, I would have gladly taken a beheading over a hanging, due to my insufficiency.

Royalty and decadence be damned, for all the good it did me in the end. Deemed a witch and a whore by Charles Brandon, the Duke of Suffolk -- and the king's best friend, nonetheless -- as well as the king's chancellor, he declared our marriage null and void, and sentenced me to live out my last days in the Tower, until he found a fit enough judgment to pass on me.

A whore and a *witch*! I could not decide which was worse. I knew the Duke and his chancellor hated me the day the king laid eyes on me, and then had a mind to make me his wife -- but such accusations were abominable, while their own abhorring, libertine indulgences went unheeded.

These were still dark, dark, ages we lived in. I had hoped humankind had gotten past the silly notions of sorcery and superstition, but I realized such things would never be wiped from the minds of uneducated, simpleminded people.

The king was a fool, and my tongue was all too quick to tell him so, sealing my doom even more. If I was to die, then I would speak freely and openly -- the time for courtesies was over.

I would have hoped my own father, who was bestowed titles and ample power himself, would have come to my aid. Unfortunately, he too, was blinded by his selfishness. Although jailed by association, he was released, but stripped of everything he was given. He cared not what happened to *me*; he only wished to save his own skin, also falsely accusing me of adultery, witchcraft and treason.

I wanted to believe he would be a *good* father, a *loving* father, but no, I was just an expendable pawn of his and my uncle's failed game to rise to power. I mattered not. My *death* mattered not. He may have walked free, but he was dead in my eyes.

Between the days of my imprisonment and execution, I gave my supplications to God, and begged for forgiveness for my sins and trespasses… and in my vexations, begged for vengeance for the betrayal of my love and devotion to the king. For it was *he* who turned a blind eye and a deaf ear to my defense. I loved him so, but it was all too obvious that love was not enough to save me from the hangman's noose. I also begged for vengeance for my father's betrayal of my love and trust in him. I was so pained with my own despair and sadness; I could not tell which betrayal was the most detestable.

I watched my brother's beheading from the Tower in which we were imprisoned, and grieved greatly for his loss. My heart felt like it was ripped from my chest. My own beloved brother, wrongfully accused, tried and sentenced. It only made me hate this unjust punishment more. And then, Mark Smeaton! For the love of God, I could not understand why *he* would be tried and beheaded. Such wonderful musical talents he had, and now they would be lost to the world forever.

I thought of my daughter, my little Elizabeth. What cruelties would Fate bestow on *her*? Who would take care of her? A cold lump formed in the pit of my stomach that made me want to vomit. The Boleyn reign was crushed.

My ladies-in-waiting did their best to soothe my broken spirit, but my resolve was slowly weakening. I heard that my execution changed from burning to beheading. Beheading would be quick, so long as the executioner was strong and steady, and hopefully I would feel no pain. But then hours later, it was decided that the king changed my beheading to *hanging*! It was as if the king could not make up his mind what to do. Did he delight in tormenting me in my last hours? Or did he want to think of the best way to make me suffer? Hanging did not offer any sense of dignity, and would be slower if my neck did not snap immediately! Yes, a beheading would have been much better. But perhaps, with me having a little neck, the noose would still do its job well.

***

As the hour of my death approached, my thinking became less sensible and more erratic. Several times, I asked God why He would allow such a punishment to befall me. Surely, there were people who led more treacherous lives than I, and still walked the earth. And here I was, judged for crimes I did not commit, and was sentenced to death. I did my best not to question my faith; perhaps something would happen that would stave off my execution, or prevent it entirely.

Such a thing never came to pass.

The time arrived, and I was led from my chambers and greeted by a cloudy May sky and a crowd of commoners bestowing their love and devotions to me for the final time. Their faces were a blur. My heart was pounding so quickly in my chest, I was sure I would faint. A mixture of a sudden heat and coldness coursed through my veins, my stomach a lump of ice. My brain was drowned in the myriad of voices coming from the people, preventing any train of thought on my end. I stared past the ocean of bodies I walked through, to the noose looming ahead, simply waiting for me.

I glanced at the Tower, once the place where I waited before my coronation, now the place that beheld my death. A face lingered in a window, watching the events, and I half-wondered if it had been Sir Thomas Wyatt. Poor, poor Thomas. Another wrongful death that would soon follow mine. I wanted to run, but retain my dignity. Even so, the guards would have caught me all too quickly. My strength availed me not during this wretched hour.

I walked up the filthy, wooden, creaking steps. Maybe I should have taken my own life. I would have spared myself the public humiliation. Besides, it looked as though God did not care either way, as He never answered my prayers.

Everyone had abandoned me. I was completely and utterly alone in this.

I paused on the last step to my pending death. The noose looked so thick, I feared my neck would slip out of it and my death would be botched. The executioner paused, as if not wanting to put it around my neck.

"Forgive me for what I must do, Your Majesty," he said to me. I merely smiled, and spoke not one word.

I looked down at the scaffolding under my feet, composed myself, and gave my final words to the crowd. The Duke was amongst them, and I seethed with hatred for him.

I could hear my heartbeat pounding in my head. All my senses were heightened -- was this what it was like before one died? The intensity of one's pending doom a stepping-stone to a higher awareness?

The hangman put the noose around my neck. The rope was dirty and harsh against my skin, making me itch. When he tightened it, I could barely swallow. The voices were suddenly unclear, their faces mishmashed in a sea of drab colors. Once I stepped onto the square hatch within the scaffold, the hatch would be dropped, and then I would swing, suspended in midair until dead.

The hangman allowed me a moment to gather the last threads of my resolve before I stepped onto the platform. If I could come back from the grave, I would give all my betrayers cause to run, as I would *never* give them a moment's rest. *Never*!

I fixed my eyes on the solid, white nothingness of the sky and cursed God for forsaking me.

The hatch was released.

I felt an intense crushing heat against my throat and the crack and snap of bone before all went black.

***

I do not know how much time had passed before I suddenly became conscious. I could breathe, and yet, I felt like I was suffocating. My movement was restricted, and I felt so very, very cold. What was this madness? Wasn't I dead? Perhaps they *thought* me dead, and buried me alive!

I felt my surroundings -- wooden, cold and damp. I was in a coffin! I needed to get out, and quickly.

I hit the wood with my fists until it broke. Cold soil and worms poured in on my face. I coughed and panicked, punching and kicking in sheer terror until shards of wood tore at my dress and scratched my skin, making me bleed.

The dirt felt so heavy around me, but it was not long before I was able to reach the surface. My head was above ground in moments, and I clawed my way through the grass and loam.

A huge, round moon hovered over me as I observed my surroundings. I had been buried on the grounds of the Chapel of St. Peter ad Vincula, merely a stone's throw from the Tower, where my brother and I were executed. And then it struck me -- I had no grave marker.

How could they do this to me? First wrongfully tried and executed, and now *this*! Buried in an unmarked grave, my body tossed into a shallow ditch as if I belonged in a potter's field! *I was the Queen of England*! I deserved far *better*! Was my brother treated in the same horrid and disrespectful fashion?

I spotted a small, silver urn at the head of my grave, tarnished by the elements. Several dead flowers hung over it. I picked up the urn and wiped away the dirt. A small piece of paper had been tucked away inside. I turned it upside down, emptying its contents, tossing aside the dead insects that fell into my palm.

On the paper was a poem:
Never there was a woman,
So fierce and yet so soft
With an unquenchable fire for life
And passions insatiable
My beloved, sweet Anne,
You are gone from this earth
And yet, I wish it were not so

I smiled. My dear, sweet Thomas. This meant he was spared his life! He was alive and well, and suddenly, I had an urge to see him. I had a feeling I would know where to find him, and made my way to Allington Castle, Thomas' home.

The night was a strange comfort to me. The more I thought about Allington, the faster it seemed I arrived there, which, I knew was humanly impossible, especially on foot, but I did not ponder over it for the time being. Too many thoughts were in my head. The hills were wide and vast, cast in a silvery-blue glow under the moon.

When I came upon Allington, I found the tree under which Thomas and I would keep each other company while he read me his poetry. Even though I was still quite a distance away, I found it strange that I could hear him as clearly as if he were standing right next to me. He was reciting one of my favorite poems of his. Such a sentimental, loving soul he was. It was a shame our predicaments prevented further courting.

I stood beside the tree. He was sitting on a branch, still talking as if I was right there listening to him, as if he was locked in the past, like things had never changed. I half-wondered if he had gone mildly insane.

I cleared my throat and read aloud the poem he left at my grave. He yelped, falling out of the tree with a heavy thud.

"Oh, Thomas!" I ran to him and tried helping him up. "I'm so sorry to have frightened you!"

"Anne... it *can't* be you! I saw you *hanged*! I saw them *bury* you!" He allowed me to help him to his feet, but when he gazed upon my face, he screamed, backing away like a madman.

"Away with you! You are a ghost! A *witch*!" His curly, brown locks in disarray, he clutched at his shirt, wide-eyed in shock.

I shook my head. "Thomas, I am no ghost, nor am I a witch. Don't be silly."

Thomas stood silent, unmoving, staring very hard at me. I spoke again.

"I was buried alive! It is not so uncommon, you know. I just never thought that it would happen to *me*." I sniffed, looking down. "I expected to be dead and gone from this world."

"But Anne... you *are* dead. Or... *something*..." I had never seen Thomas so fearful of anything before.

I laughed at him. "I helped you up, did I not? I am speaking to you now, am I not? Ghosts cannot do such things."

The tone of my chiding voice must have helped Thomas finally regain his courage, and he took a cautious step towards me. He touched my cheek, cringed, and then took a step back again. "But, Anne... y-your face..."

"What about my face?" I demanded, as my hands flew to my cheeks, feeling for any deformities.

He took me by the hand and led me to the moat surrounding his home, and pointed to it.

"Look."

I glanced at him and smirked before I fell to my knees, bent over, and peered at my reflection.

My skin was as pale as the moon. My dark hair had long streaks of white as bright as my skin. However, the most horrifying thing was my eyes. They were the color of blood.

It took all the strength in me not to scream as I touched my lips and around my throat. I could still see the rope burns on my neck.

"Dear God in heaven, what has happened to me?"

Thomas simply shook his head. "If you weren't a witch when I knew you, then you are definitely one *now*."

"I've made no pact with any devil or demon! *How* has this

happened?"

The moment I said it, I knew. The realization struck me like an arrow to the heart.

It happened the very instant I denounced God -- *right before my death.*

Smite me for such foolishness!

This was my *curse*, my punishment directly from our Lord Almighty! I *was* dead! A demoness of the night. My soul was damned for eternity!

But then, I thought it over. If I *were* cursed, then I would take full advantage of it!

Without a word, I raced away from him and down the road, my new objective now getting to my own home, Hever Castle. Hever was well a ways from Allington, but my current mind frame knew of no long distance between the two castles.

"Anne? *Anne!*" Thomas called after me. "Where are you going? Wait for me!"

"I'm going home, Thomas," I replied, not bothering to look back at him.

I had spanned the lands with such ease in my new form -- what would have taken a few hours by carriage, I managed to do in mere minutes. I crossed the bridge that hovered over the moat, but was stopped by the heavy iron portcullis. Any servants would be asleep, and if they saw me, they too, would be too terrified to let me in.

If I could somehow raise the portcullis! The lever was well out of my reach, behind the gate, and I cursed it. I wanted to get to my father with such ferocity; I began to hear the clanking of chains. Confused, I saw the gate slowly rising. The lever was moving of its *own accord*. Was *I* the cause of that? My very thoughts put into action by an unseen force?

It did not rise completely, just enough for me to stoop under the bars. Fine with me.

I searched the castle from top to bottom. No one was around. The house was as dark and empty as my soul. I lit a candle, went to my chambers, and sat on my bed, pondering what to do next.

On my bed stand, I found my prayer book, and picked it up. It was old and worn, the cover frayed with use. I flipped to the back of the book,

noticing a few words I had scrawled across the blank pages:
The time will come.

I must have had a very morbid sense of humor at the time, as I also had sketched corpses climbing out of their graves, and titled the drawing, "The Resurrection of the Dead". My eyes rested on the drawing for a moment, my mind spinning again with devious and abominable thoughts. I must have stayed that way for quite a while, for, before I knew it, I heard horse's hooves approaching the castle. I continued to listen as Thomas' heavy footsteps eventually ascended the stairs and reached my bedchamber.

He was sweating, the candlelight making his chest glisten. Standing in the doorstop, he stared at me, panting, still unnerved.

I retained my composure, not wanting to frighten him any further. I was surprised he had followed me; perhaps it was the sheer fascination of seeing me alive, and in the state I was in, which overtook his rationality.

"Do you know where my brother is buried?" I asked him gently.

Thomas seemed reluctant to answer, so I asked him again as I got up, approaching him almost seductively.

"Oh Thomas, don't be afraid of me. After all we've shared, and all we've done... especially in this room..." I gave him a smile, reached out, and touched his face. He swooned, entranced by my voice. "Tell me where he is."

Thomas wrapped his arms around my waist, his warmth feeling so good against my cold body. He leaned into me, and I rubbed my face against his neck.

A strange, primitive urge overcame me. I inhaled the musky scent of his skin, and ran my fingers through his soft hair. I trailed my tongue over his neck before I bit down deeply. Thomas shuddered and cried out as his blood flowed into my mouth. I do not know what came over me, what possessed me to do such a thing, but when I tasted his essence; I knew it would be vital to my new existence. It felt instinctual, as if I had known how to do this all along.

I let Thomas go, and he stumbled before dropping to the floor. He was in a daze when he glanced up at me, with several bloodstains on his collar, but nonetheless, no longer frightened.

"I'll show you where he is, my dear, sweet Anne," he replied, getting up and making his way downstairs and to his horse, which was tied to the bridge.

As I approached the animal, it began to snort and whinny. Being whatever it was I had become, the beast had no desire to be near something so unnatural.

I stared the creature in its eyes and commanded it to calm down. Once I had it under control, Thomas helped me onto his horse, and we made our way back to where my brother was buried. Knowing that I held a strange, supernatural power, I hoped that what I had in mind to do to my brother would come to fruition.

***

We arrived right back at the chapel, and I laughed. I didn't think they'd put him in the same resting place as I.

Thomas gave me a funny look "What is so amusing?"

I shook my head as an answer as he helped me down off his horse. I wandered the misty grounds, wondering if George would have an unmarked grave as well. I stared at the many markers -- simple wooden crosses with one's name etched into them.

"George, where are you?" I whispered into the wind. "Let me find you... please, let me find you..."

Thomas watched me carefully as I continued to wander the grounds. I stopped when I found George's marker, and fell to my knees once more. George had been so close to my own grave, and I didn't even realize it.

I lay on the ground beside him, and wept as I ran my hands through the soil he now lay under. I heard Thomas come up from behind me.

"My dear, beloved George," I whispered. "Rise with me. Rise with me and help me to avenge our deaths! Help me with this task, dear brother, so we can find some peace at last."

The ground under me began to rumble, and I sat up. Not sure if I was hearing things or not, I put my ear to the ground.

Thumping. Dear God in heaven, he *was* trying to rise!

My strange, unearthly plea was working! Such a joy it was to find I could speak such things into existence!

But then, I cringed in terror. *George had been beheaded.*

I stood up, not knowing what to expect, and turned to Thomas. He lost all color in his face, and began backing away.

"What devilry is this, Anne? What are you doing to your brother?"

I could not answer, because I did not know what to say. I had a power beyond that of a king *or* queen, and I laughed again in dark triumph.

"Come dear brother, come! Walk with me once again!" I raised my arms to the indigo sky, willing him to rise with all my might.

The ground began to move and pulse, and a withered, deathly white hand protruded from the soil. Thomas became weak at the knees and fell to the ground.

I took a step back, my heart feeling cold with dread. "How long has it been, Thomas?"

His voice was shaking. "W-what?"

"How *long*, Thomas? How long has it been since our deaths?"

"Days," he answered. "I've lost count of them in my grief."

I had no idea what George would look like, and I was not sure if he was suffering the same evil fate as I. As I watched his body slowly rise, I nearly fainted.

There would be no way he could walk with me... without his head.

I swallowed. His body sitting erect in the dirt, it waited for my next command.

"Thomas..." I started. "Fetch his head."

He gave me an incredulous look. "F-fetch his *what*?"

"Fetch... his... *head*," I repeated, punctuating each word. "Surely they buried his body together with his head."

"Perhaps," he answered, sweating in nervousness. "I do not know for sure."

"Well? Go ahead, then! I need you to look."

He grimaced before walking over to George's grave, and knelt down. Not surprisingly, George's body was still wearing the same torn and bloody shirt he had worn at his execution.

"This goes against all that is Godly, Anne. This is the work of darker forces!"

"I *am* that darker force," I answered, then looked down. "And I've brought it upon myself."

Thomas dug through the loosened dirt and drew back as if something had stung him.

"I felt it," he told me. "But -- I cannot bear to pick it up!"

"Ponce," I mumbled under my breath, and waved him away. I thrust my hands into the soil, feeling small, cold, squirming worms tickling my skin. I touched hair next, and pulled George's head up from his grave.

His skin was an ashen gray, waxy looking and worm-eaten. His eye sockets pooled with maggots that spilled onto my stained, torn dress. I could feel his hair begin to tear away from his scalp, so I quickly placed his head upon his neck, holding it there, as I willed his head and body to be whole again. After a minute of focus, I took my hands away. The only thing that remained was the mark from the executioner's axe.

It was then that Thomas groaned and fainted.

I gripped George's shoulders. "George... George, my dear brother... it's Anne!"

Soil and insects cascaded from his mouth as a voice that was gravelly and unlike his own escaped his decaying lips.

"Aaannnne...."

I laughed again and embraced the foul corpse of my dead brother. I was already beyond sanity and sensibility, and I had not a care in the world. I wanted my revenge, and, damn it all to hell, I *would* have it!

I thought back to the words written in my prayer book.

The time will come, indeed.

Chapter Two

Searching for Smeaton was not as easy. Thomas had no clue as to where he was buried, and my guess was that he would have been buried among commoners. Commoner's graves were aplenty, scattered all over the fields of England.

Well, I was the queen, albeit a supernatural one, and it looked as though I could do whatever I wanted.

I felt uncomfortable with George lumbering about us. He was not at all limber. To my dismay, I also discovered I could not reverse the process of his decomposition, which seemed a bit of a paradox, considering I was somehow able to weld his head to his neck. But for now, I would take what I could get.

Thomas and I helped George onto the horse, and Thomas led the creature as he and I walked. My mind was still spinning, trying to think of where they could have possibly buried Smeaton.

"Why do you need him?" Thomas asked me. Since he was now going to be my footman, there was no harm in talking to him. Besides, with our amorous past, that made it all the more easier for him to assist me.

"He was wronged just as much as my brother," I answered, as we passed a field of wildflowers. "And he was a very dear friend to me."

"Many men were your friends." He gave a smirk.

"But none were as dear to my heart as my brother, you, and Smeaton."

"I'm glad to know I was not forgotten about entirely while you were queen."

I turned and faced him. "I could never forget about you, Thomas."

We walked a while before he spoke again.

"You know, whatever the outcome of all of this is, no matter how tragic… if I should die before it's all over, please don't do *that* to me." He gestured to George, who was still sitting silently upon his horse. Something was leaking from his body, a greenish black fluid of some sort. Neither one of us mentioned the unpleasant odors emanating from him; that was to be expected from a corpse now walking above ground.

I sniffed as a reply, since I was at a loss for words.

We did not travel far before I instinctively stopped and stared at what appeared to be a crowded little cemetery in the middle of nowhere. The air was damp, and a light fog had settled over the lands. A few huge oaks loomed over the stones, but the rest of the land was vacant. I walked towards the graves, Thomas and George trailing behind me.

"Smeaton… Smeaton.…" I chanted as I approached the markers. "Come out, come out, and show yourself. Come forward and share in my revenge…"

By the time I reached the cemetery, I spotted Smeaton's headless body sitting up in his shallow grave. I smiled.

"There," I pointed to a row in the back. "There lies Smeaton."

"Sitting up sounds more like it," Thomas mumbled, and I frowned at his poor joke.

"Well, find his head! I'll have to do for him what I did for George."

Thomas made a noise of disgust and plodded onward.

I liked the glow that the moon cast on all the little white crosses in the field. It gave a haunting yet serene quality to the scenery. All these souls laid to rest in such a quiet little spot, away from the dank slums of London, away from the unquiet busyness of the world. Forever asleep, forever at peace…

And I unintentionally forbade myself such an option. This thought nagged at me, but I continued to ignore it.

Thomas found Smeaton's head, and in a much worse state than George's. It appeared as if he had undergone some torture, as what was left of the skin on his forehead showed signs of being burned.

The maggots and insects were still plentiful as I placed Smeaton's head upon his neck and willed his body to become whole. Like George, only the mark of the axe remained on his neck after I was done.

"If I were to write about any of this, I would be deemed a madman until I died," Thomas said to himself.

"Things like this need not be written about," I replied, helping Smeaton out of his grave. He clothing was just as soiled as George's was, if not in more disrepair. His shirt was torn in several areas -- possibly the result of whip marks -- while exposing his decaying back and chest.

Several worms continued spilling out from between his ribs and rotted insides, and his mobility was just as hindered as my brother's.

"Smeaton?" I asked. "Can you speak?"

Although eyeless, he focused his dirt-filled sockets on me.

"Anne..." His voice was also not his own; it was whispery and raspy, snatched away by the claws of death -- or the axe simply left his throat in as much a ragged condition as George's. "What... have... you... done?"

Seeing black soil and insects spill from a dead man's mouth twice in one night was too much, even for me.

I blinked. "Smeaton, what do you mean? I have awakened you from a premature slumber! You, my brother and I shall have our revenge on those who have treated us unfairly."

"I know... I was wronged... but I committed... myself to death. I do not wish... to walk the earth anymore... Not like this... Put me back, Anne... Return me... to the ground!"

I was taken aback at his statement. "Smeaton, my friend! Surely you can't mean that!"

"Put me back!" He took a step forward as if to frighten me, and I fumed.

"How *dare* you! I have gone out of my way to bring you to life... and you want to be put *back*?" I took a step back from him. "Fine! Then GO!"

I waved him off, an invisible force throwing him backwards, making him land in his shallow grave with a heavy thump. His head dislocated from his body on impact, rolling a few feet away from him. I heard Thomas gasp, but he said not a word.

I turned, walking back to him and George.

"You -- you're just going to leave him there?" he asked. "Won't someone see his open grave as sacrilege?"

"No one cares about commoners' graves," I spat. "If anything, they'll believe that he was dug up by wild animals to be eaten."

Thomas's expression was pained, but he remained silent.

***

I do not know how long we walked, but a faint light began to show in the horizon. Dawn was approaching.

"We'll need a place to hide," I told Thomas. "No one can know about me or my brother's existence. And I need time to gather my senses."

"You can hide at my castle. It would not make sense for you to go to Hever. Not now, anyways."

"Oh, I *do* intend on going there, Thomas. I need pay my father a visit." I gave him a cruel grin.

"Your father?! But why--?"

I put a cold finger to his lips, and his eyes widened in surprise.

"Ask no questions, Thomas. All will be answered soon."

A streak of sunlight appeared over the hilltops, and I closed my eyes, welcoming its warmth.

Then I became too hot. I felt like I was scorching. Suddenly, my hand caught on fire from out of nowhere. I screamed, draping my tattered cape over it.

The heat was so intense! It felt like I would explode!

"Thomas!" I shrieked, and he covered me with his coat, rushing me under a tree.

"What is *wrong* with me?" I asked, flipping off the coat when I was in the shade. Wisps of smoke escaped from my clothing, vanishing into the air. "The sun feels like fire against my skin, and burns me like parchment to a flame!"

"See? It is further proof that you have become a creature of darkness! No heavenly thing would be bothered by the light of day. You must cower from the sun in the coldness of the night!"

"A Boleyn does not *cower*," I sneered, tossing his coat at him in anger. "*Now* what will I do?"

He draped his coat back over me. "We must hurry. Allington is not that far now. Just over that glen." He pointed in the distance.

"I'll meet you there," I said, and took off. It was so much easier traveling alone.

I stayed under our favorite tree in the shade until he showed up with my brother. I was glad to see the sun did not affect George, but his condition still had not improved. Now, seeing him in the light, he looked more grotesque than I had ever imagined. Abomination, ha! That word was such an understatement.

Thomas led us to a vacant servant's quarters where we stayed well hidden until nightfall. It gave me plenty of time to reorganize my thoughts and figure out my next move.

I lie on a bed in the tiny room, while George sat in a chair, stiff and quiet, his putrid limbs lying perfectly on their armrests. Occasionally, larvae would fall from his body and plop to the floor in little, wet splats. This thing was not like him at all, and immediately I was so sorry for what I did to him. My brother was lively, talkative and handsome! Everything that this dead body was the *opposite* of.

Because that was all he was. A dead body, brought to life by *me*. Me, a queen turned martyr, turned demon-of-the-night.

But what a *un*-life George now had. He possessed no real spirit or soul. George may have been conscious, but he could not think for himself, only what I commanded of him.

I could not let George remain like this. Just one more day, and then, I *had* to put him back to rest.

I looked at my burned hand. It looked so skeletal -- charred, blackened flesh stuck to red chunks of muscle and bone -- so I willed it to heal. It took a while, but by the time I had fully rested, my hand was completely rejuvenated.

Upon my awakening, I was startled to see Smeaton standing at the foot of my bed.

He bowed at me and gave a charming smile. "Your Majesty."

It took a moment for me to figure out what was going on. Being able to look right through him, it was all too easy to deduct I was seeing his ghost.

I gave him a smirk. "What made you change your mind?" I asked as I sat up.

He pointed at poor George, who had not budged since he sat down.

"Did you *really* think I'd want to roam the earth looking like *that*? How would you expect me to charm the ladies without my dashing smile and captivating wit? At least my handsome looks prevail in *this* form. Dead flesh has too many disadvantages!"

Even so, I could still see the faint image of the axe's mark on his phantom neck.

"You still won't be able to charm *any* lady, once they see you walk through *walls*."

"Or *see through you*, period," Thomas added. We turned, noticing him standing in the doorway, looking at us. "Come to join the hellish party, Smeaton?"

"I can *never* pass up a good party." He smiled, threw back his black hair, and tucked a violin under his chin. He played a few quick, cheerful notes, and when he was done, I clapped for him.

"Beautiful as always," I commented, and he bowed before me. "It's good to hear your music once again."

Thomas noticed my hand. "You're all healed, I see."

"It seems a good rest will do that." I rubbed it and wiggled my fingers.

George gave a deep, guttural cough, and a few maggots projected from his mouth. Smeaton flinched.

"*Not* attractive... and I rest my case!"

"You still didn't answer my question," I said, folding my arms. "What made you change your mind? Back at your grave, I considered you out of my little game."

"Dear Anne, you gave me quite a bit to reconsider," he replied. "And I *enjoy* your games, no matter how morbid. Besides, once it's over, I'll be able to rest permanently!" He glanced at me and cleared his throat. "That is, if you'll permit me."

I gave him a big smile. "Thank you Smeaton. If you were solid, I'd embrace you."

Thomas snorted and chuckled to himself, so I shot him a look. He gave a mock cough and looked away.

"Well, Your Majesty, what's on the agenda for tonight?"

"Actually... Her Majesty she is no longer," Thomas mumbled.

I whipped around. "*What?*"

"Well, aside from your marriage being made null and void right before your execution, once you were dead, Jane Seymour became engaged to His Highness."

I screamed in a rage, and all three men jumped.

"Licentious *bastard*!" I hissed. "I'm not even dead a whole week and he plans to wed the next wench in line! I *knew* my father's plans to rise the Boleyns to power would be detrimental to us!" I put a hand to my forehead in disgust, and tried calming my nerves before I spoke again.

"I'm going to Hever, Thomas. *Now*. And Smeaton, I have a fun task for you to do."

"Anything, Lady Anne. Say the word."

I stepped up to him and gave a sultry smile. "Play your violin," I said. "Play it loud and play it long. Let your melodies echo throughout the corridors of Whitehall Palace until the early dawn."

Smeaton looked unsure. "Hmmm. I've never tried playing that long before."

I put my hands on my hips. "You're a *ghost* now, Smeaton. You could go on for all *eternity* if you so desired."

He laughed. "As you wish, My Lady," he replied, dissipating right before our eyes.

I helped George to his feet. "Come, dear brother. It's time to see our father, now." I turned to Thomas and grinned. "--And we're going to need your horse again."

Chapter Three

"*You don't* have to come with us, you know," I told Thomas as he helped me mount his horse once more. George held onto my waist for support. Trying to ignore the dripping bugs rolling into my lap from the wormholes in his arms, I brushed them off. "It might be better if father doesn't see you with us, anyway. You have been through enough tortures and trials because of me. God forbid he tries to accuse *you* of witchcraft."

Thomas paused, thinking it over. "All right, Anne. I'll stay."

"I'll return when I need your help again. Besides, my shelter is here with you."

He smiled and bowed at me before I took off.

I had to be careful while riding with George. A few times, I was afraid he would fall off, and slowed the horse down for his sake. I ran through my mind all the things I wanted to say to our father, having the feeling I would forget half of them by the time I met him face to face. But then, my anger overcame my trepidation. He could do nothing to hurt me; on the contrary, it would be the other way around.

We came upon Hever Castle, and I left Thomas' horse under the same oak tree Henry once courted me under. Another memory I could have done without. I helped George down next, and together, we made a slow, meticulous walk to the bridge and stood before the portcullis. I commanded the gate to rise, and without hesitation, I heard the chains clanking as it rose for us. I ushered George forward.

We entered our home, and only a few candles were alight. At least I knew he was here this time.

Making our way through the hallways and corridors, I was not surprised to find the place so dark and desolate. More than likely, he lost many of his servants, due to his lack of funding and loss of position at the palace.

George was making a mess everywhere he stepped. Between the rancid fluids leaking from his every orifice -- natural or worm-made -- the insect larvae seemed *endless*. But secretly, I grinned. Let our father have at *that* for a moment!

He was here *somewhere*, and I would not leave until we found him.

We discovered our father in the dining hall, sitting alone at the table, a few candles lighting the abysmal, cold room. He was having his supper, while dealing with a fit of coughs in-between chews. It sounded like he was getting sick, but I pitied him not.

I took George's hand. "Are you ready?" I whispered, and he nodded at me.

With a single thought, I transported us in a flash. We now stood right behind him, as silent as the grave. The only noise was an occasional drip that came from George's body, but it went unnoticed.

What *did not* go unnoticed was George's foul smell. Our father lifted his head, taking a whiff of the air, and then fanned the front of his nose. He tried to go back to eating, but he plopped down the piece of chicken leg he was eating, probably nauseated from the stench, and put his napkin over his mouth. He coughed some more, this time out of disgust.

I could not contain myself any longer and laughed, my voice echoing throughout the chamber. He gave a noise of shock, turned around, and screamed, jumping up out of his seat, knocking it over. The clamor resounded through the stone room.

"I fear your odors have upset our dear father, George," I said sarcastically, giving a pointed grin.

Our father could not speak at first. No words could come to mind at seeing his dead children standing before him.

"Blasphemy... *blasphemeeee*...!" he finally blurted out, making the sign of the Holy Cross over himself. His eyes were wide, and he trembled so hard, he collapsed into another chair. "Almighty Father in heaven! What is this madness? Who are you?" he demanded.

"*What*? How can you not recognize your dear *Anne* and beloved son *George*?" I snapped. "But again, you still found it hard to recognize me, even before my death!"

"Anne... Anne..." he stuttered, and then glanced over to George. "This cannot be real! This is the Devil's work!"

"Not the Devil's work father, but the work of *your own two hands*!"

He shook his head in defiance. "I am no witch! I could *never* do something as repulsive as *this*!" He tried waving us off, as if *that* would do him any good.

"Ah, but all your past actions have *led up* to this. If not for your desire to rise in power, I may have never died for your failed plans! *George* would have never died! You USED me, father!"

"No!"

"YES! *You used me*! But answer me this -- was it all worth it in the end? *Was it*? To lose your children to your own greed?!"

He closed his eyes and began reciting The Lord's Prayer, and I hissed at him, breaking his concentration. When he opened them, he jumped again, as I was merely inches from his face. The candlelight reflected the terror in his eyes, and the anger in mine.

"Tell me something, father... did you even love me as a daughter, or was I just a pawn to you?"

He slid to the floor, and dropped to his knees, clasping his hands together. "I beseech you, daughter, please have mercy on me, lecherous wretch that I am!"

"Get *up*," I snapped, grabbing his collar and hauling him up to his feet. "Your words are *meaningless* to me. Look upon your daughter -- what *you* have created!"

"You... are not... my daughter! She... is... *dead*!"

I smacked him, knocking him back to the floor. He crumpled. As he looked up at me, he wiped the blood from his mouth.

"Did *that* feel dead to you?!" I yelled. "I *trusted* you, father! I *loved* you! But you betrayed me in my greatest hour of need! You LIED about my convictions to save your own skin! You didn't even stay to see my *execution*! For God's sake, man... your own *daughter*!" Tears welled up in my eyes, and he saw something so great, so deadly in them -- besides their red hue -- that he began backing away from me, and actually summoned up the courage to try and defend himself.

"Anne, you cannot blame me for everything. If you hadn't lost the king's son, *none* of this would have come to pass! We'd *all* still be at the castle, alive and happy!"

I shrieked so loud, both my father and George covered their ears.

"HOW *DARE* YOU BLAME ME!" I bellowed. "The king's *wenching* upset me enough to miscarry!"

"And I told you... it's natural for a king to take a mistress, especially when his wife is with child! It is the duty of a queen to overlook such things! Your *jealousies* are to blame for our downfall, Anne, not *me*!"

I grabbed him by his neck and raised him off his feet. I had enough of his foolish talk. "It was YOU who pushed me to get into the king's good graces! YOU who wanted more power! I *had* a love father, and I was *so* content with him! To become a queen was not something I had a mind to do!" I gave his neck a squeeze, and he gasped for air.

Father clawed at my hand as he tried to speak. "Please Anne... *forgive me*! Forgive your broken, old father! What can I possibly do to make things up to you?"

I tilted my head to the side. "*Make it up to me*? Have you gone daft? I'm DEAD father; there IS no way to make it up to me!" I dropped him and beckoned to George, who shuffled towards him. Blurting another noise of fear, he scooted away again. I started to wonder if he feared George more than he feared me.

"The time has come *dear father*," I said with a snide grin. "No apologies can be accepted."

I swooped down and fought against his fearful struggling as I bared my fangs and bit into his neck.

***

Despite it all, I decided to let him live. Killing him now would have only lessened the fun of torturing him again later. I did, however, leave him substantially weaker than he was. Moreover, all George had to do was to take a step towards him, and our father would start in with a fit of hellish screaming that echoed throughout all of Hever Castle.

Getting revenge was quite easy, and oh, so much *fun*...

I told George to stay with our father, and keep him company for a while. As I rode Thomas' horse away from Hever, I could still hear my father's screams of, "Get away from me! *Get awaaaay*!"

The night was still young when I arrived back at Allington. Thomas had fallen asleep in his bedchamber, trying to wait up for me. I sat at the foot of his bed, watching him sleep.

"You said you'd love me always," I whispered. "But, where once was love, love is no more. Where there was light, there is an unending darkness. All is lost, sweet Thomas. All is lost." I covered my mouth to prevent myself from sobbing, but a few tears escaped, running down my cheeks.

Regaining my composure, I let him sleep, and decided to make my way to Whitehall Palace. The night was not yet over, and I would make the most of it.

***

I left Thomas' horse tied up at his stables. The poor beast had done quite a bit of running for all of us. My travels were swifter without the creature, so it was not long before I arrived at court. Things were winding down, and most folks were calling it a night.

I spotted one of Jane's ladies-in-waiting wenching with a member of the Privy Council right at the dining table, and no one seemed to notice, or politely ignored it. The king was nowhere to be found. Several others were drunk, talking loudly, laughing and singing as a new court musician played on. As much as I admired music and all forms of art, this new musician was not as good as Smeaton. And speaking of him, I wondered if he was doing as I had asked.

No better way to find out than to roam the halls.

I had no doubt that the king would have given Jane my old chambers, but, on second thought, since he hated me so, he probably had given her a new room altogether. I took my chances and went to my former chambers first, which were empty and unused. Sighing, I ventured further.

Then I heard it. A violin was playing in the distance, and I grinned. I would know Smeaton's gay music anywhere. I followed the sound, hoping he was cavorting near our enemies, driving them insane with his phantom melodies.

Knowing I did not have the convenience of being a specter, I draped my hood over my head, keeping my face well out of view. I still looked too suspicious, but it was better than showing my face outright.

Smeaton's music led me to a hall that two frazzled guards quickly walked down, passing me as if I was not even there, mumbling something about "the music with no musician". The violin was so loud where I stood, it was no wonder why the guards looked frightened. I laughed at them.

"You can stop now, Smeaton," I said, and he materialized before me.

"I hope I'm doing a good job." He flashed a handsome smile at me.

I glanced down the hall, grinning. "You definitely gave those guards a good fright."

Behind the door Smeaton stood in front of, I could hear noises of carnal pleasure. The tone of the male voice sounded a lot like--

"His Majesty is within, with a mistress, no doubt." Smeaton rolled his eyes. "How I miss those days…"

"Play louder," I snapped, and he quickly obeyed.

After a few seconds, Henry gave a noise of annoyance. "Whoever's playing that damned, bloody violin will have their fingers *crushed*!"

We heard footsteps, so Smeaton laughed and vanished. My unnatural speed had me down at the end of the hallway before Henry even opened the door. Looking around and seeing no one, he seemed confused until Smeaton played his music again. This time, Henry looked unnerved. He stood out in the hallway, bold and naked, looking, listening, appearing even more befuddled. Frustrated, he went back in and slammed the door. I stood in front of his chambers once more, and Smeaton stopped playing.

"His Majesty is quite perturbed! Do you want me to start moaning and rattling chains next?"

"Your moaning would sound more like a man who's enjoying a woman," I answered with a smirk. "That wouldn't frighten *anyone*. But have you found out where Jane sleeps?"

"Not yet, My Lady. Shall we find her together?"

"Yes. But first…" I produced a bouquet of yellow daffodils from within my cloak and dropped them at the king's chamber door. "Now, off we go."

***

We were unlucky in finding Jane's chambers that night, but no matter. I had no reason to rush things. Torture was best when done slowly.

The court was quiet, and the guards were doing their nightly rounds. I would have to be stealthier now, although there were plenty of places within the castle in which I could hide.

I wondered if the king had found my little gift, and made a trip back to his quarters. There they still lay on the floor. Angered, I pounded on his door and screamed his name. *That* would surely startle him.

When I was well out of sight, I waited for him to make a move. In seconds, he threw his door open, then looked down at his feet. He stared at the daffodils, afraid to pick them up. Then quickly, he bent down, grabbed them, and took off. Thank the heavens he was clothed this time. His whore must have been long gone.

I followed after him, my footsteps untraceable. When he came across a guard, Henry shoved him against a wall to get his attention. I sniffed. Still a bully, as always.

"Whose idea was it to put these daffodils at my door?" he yelled, shoving the flowers in the guard's face. "Is this someone's idea of a sick joke? I'll beat them down like a *dog*!"

"I have no clue as to who could have done this, Your Majesty." The guard looked puzzled at the king's anger towards him.

"Find *out*," Henry snapped, throwing the flowers at his chest. "They're impersonating Anne's voice, trying to scare me, so obviously, it's a female. Perhaps one of her supporters!"

I could not help it. I laughed again, my disembodied voice making both of them jump. The sound echoed through the hall, and the guard became more panicky than Henry.

"First the music, and now this," he mumbled. The king whipped around.

"What are you talking about?"

"We heard music playing… a-a violin! However, there was no one around! I heard the music playing just as close as you are to me! Ask Anthony, he'll tell you the same thing!"

"I shall," Henry replied, storming off to find the second guard.

"The time will come," I said aloud, and upon hearing my voice, with no person to match it, the first guard's eyes widened in stark-raving fear as he ran down the corridor.

This was too much! I grinned as I heard Smeaton's laughter again before he appeared.

"What a romp this is, indeed!" he told me. "Who knew being dead would be so much fun! How much longer will we keep at this?"

"Until I see fit to stop," I answered plainly. "But we'll continue my game another night. I have to fetch my brother from our home. Meet us at Thomas' again tomorrow."

"Fare thee well, My Lady," he replied, giving my hand an ethereal kiss before disappearing.

***

Upon my arrival at Hever, I noticed the portcullis was still up, allowing me entrance without hassle. As I walked down the cold, lifeless corridors, I came to the dining hall, the candles upon the table nearly out. I did not see my father or George at first, only hearing a faint, weak voice, still chanting, "*Go awaaaay...*"

In a corner of the hall, barely aglow with the candles' flames, my brother stood, hovered over our father, who was huddled in a ball, staring into George's eyeless sockets. The only thing that filled them was the continuously squirming vermin. Every time my father tried to make a move, George thrust his arms forward as if to stop him. Father had already relieved his water and his bowels, as the horrid odors of feces and urine were in the air.

I walked up to them, and father did not even acknowledge me. On further observation, father's gaze looked as if it were far away, his eyes not truly focused on George, but looking *through* him. He was a mess of drool and senseless ramblings now, and I shook my head.

"Dear George, you never gave him a chance to move *at all*?"

George slowly shook his head, and I could hear the tearing of sinew and muscle within his carcass in that one, subtle movement.

"Come George," I said gently, leading him away by his shoulder. "I think our work here is done."

I looked behind me and saw father watching us, his austere, cold persona long gone. In a way, our father really *was* dead.

***

Since I did not have the horse for George's benefit, we made the trek back to Allington on foot, not that it mattered to me. I do not think it bothered George either; it was just that he moved so slowly. Besides, the long walk gave me a lot of time to think.

The second night of this raving lunacy was diverting in its own morose way, but already, I was tiring of the charade. With some of my anger relieved, my tenacity in seeing the rest of my plans through was dwindling. I really did not wish to continue living out the rest of this new life looking the way I did, and being what I was, but still, I had to fulfill my promise to George in returning him to his grave.

By the time we arrived back at Allington, light was appearing in the sky. We got to the servant's quarters, where Thomas was waiting for us. He was sitting at a table, writing something by candlelight.

"Anne!" He jumped up and ran to me, embracing me. I was surprised he did not flinch this time. Had he gotten used to the insanity of it all, already? "I was afraid you wouldn't make it in time."

"Well, I had to keep George's pace," I answered. "I can't travel swiftly with a partner, remember? And I wasn't about to leave him alone." I sat on the bed, and George resumed his position in the chair. "What were you writing?" I gestured to the papers on the table.

"I was thinking of creating a satire," he answered. "A parody about death."

"And what, pray tell, do you find so amusing about it?"

"Well, I've had *plenty* of inspiration as of late," he answered with that smile that I so dearly loved.

Thomas sat next to me, a somber look on his face. "You may have believed me to be asleep, but I heard what you said earlier. About love being lost." He looked down at his lap. "Were you talking about me, or yourself?"

"Both of us," I whispered. "Our lives changed so drastically once my father charged me with attending court to gain the king's favor." I looked away, my face growing hot.

"Despite everything that came between us, and the things I may have said, I *never* lost my love for you, Anne. I loved you then -- and I *still* love you now."

"I am *not* a living being, Thomas!" I snapped, getting up. "I have no idea what I am, besides being a bitch of the Devil. How can you still be so besotted with me?"

"Anne, *stop it*," he chided, getting up as well. "You still have that same fire, that same spirit, wit and charm that makes you... *you*." He tilted my face, meeting my gaze. "Yes, Anne, I still love you."

Our lips met, his mouth so warm and soft against my deathly coldness. However, I welcomed it just the same, and he pressed his body to mine.

Our kissing would have gone further if I had not stopped.

"My brother..." I said in between soft panting.

Thomas glanced over my shoulder. "He's not even *looking*, Anne."

"But Thomas... he's still in here *with* us."

He gave a little sigh of frustration, grabbed a sheet off the bed, and began to walk over to George. I knew exactly what he was about to do, and stopped him.

"Don't you *dare*," I said, sounding stern, grabbing his wrist. "He's not some piece of furniture you can just *cover up*."

"Aaanne!" he whined.

"Not another word. You and George were good friends. Even *I* don't think he'd appreciate you covering him for *your* benefit."

Thomas smirked. "Sorry George," he said, before tossing the sheet onto the floor. George didn't respond, only tilted his head ever so slightly.

I sighed and walked over to a window, looking out of it. Sunlight touched the hills once more, and I was stuck indoors again until nightfall. I had another busy night ahead of me, as I still had a few more family members to meet… as well as say goodbye to.

Chapter Four

When night fell, I awoke from my daytime slumber to find Thomas sprawled out on the bed beside me. I sat up slowly, so not to disturb him. I was not in much of a talkative mood.

I beckoned George to follow me, so he got up, and I could hear more cracks and snaps resonating from within the hollowed husk of his corpse. Most of the maggots and insects had finally dried out and died, and now they were but mere grubby piles scattered around on the floor.

I took George's dry, bony hand and led him outside, his footsteps very sluggish, and his general movement more strenuous.

"I'm so sorry George, for having done this to you," I said, as we spoke under the moonlight. "This wasn't what I wanted for you. I was blinded with rage for what was done to us. My vengeance was so great; I could not see the harm I was doing to you in the process. I hope you can forgive me."

George put his leathery, cold palm on top of mine, and tried to speak.

"Nothing.... to... forgive."

Tears came to my eyes. Even though he was this disgusting *thing* of abhorrence, he was also once my brother. My best friend. The one whom I could go to for anything. The one whom I could talk to about any problem I had.

"Oh George," I said, embracing his corpse. It took a moment, but his cracking, splitting joints and drying muscles bent just enough to give me a stiff embrace in return. "It's time for you to rest again."

Knowing that his movements were more hindered than the last time, the whole night would be lost to me if we walked from here to the chapel. I hitched a cart to Thomas' horse, wrapped my brother in burlap cloth, and had him lay down in it. I mounted the horse, and took off as fast as I could. I just hoped he would not fall to pieces before we arrived -- the ride would be a terribly bumpy one for him.

When the Tower was in my sights, I sighed in relief and continued onward to the chapel. I led the horse under a tree and hopped down, then hurried to the cart to check on George.

He still was in one piece, and none the worse for wear. I helped him out of the cart and walked him to his grave.

The lands were foggy again, the air damp. It took a moment to locate where he had been buried. Once we found it, I would have sworn I felt a sense of relief emanating from him.

His grave had not even been tampered with. It looked the same as when he had left it.

George climbed back into his splintered, broken coffin and lay down, placing his hands over his chest.

I held one his hands and smiled bravely for him.

"We had fun, didn't we?" I asked. He slowly nodded a reply.

"I release you from your ungodly bonds," I whispered. "Rest in peace, my dear brother."

A chill drifted in the air as I felt his spirit lift itself from its decaying prison, and the dark magic that held his body together was no more. I watched as his head suddenly fell to the side, separated from him once again, a grim reminder of the fate that had been bestowed upon him.

Choking back sobs, I gathered up the soil surrounding his grave, and pushed it back on top of him. This task was *so* much harder than bringing him back to life.

Once I was done, I sat there quietly for a moment, reflecting back on our happier times…the times before we became figureheads of political power. I never realized how dangerous it could be for us to be given such positions of high standing. If I knew it would lead up to this, I would have quickly refused my father's charge without a second thought.

"You've said your goodbyes, I see," a voice came from behind me. I turned, and could barely notice Smeaton amidst the fog of the churchyard.

"How did you know where to find me?"

"When I visited Allington, I saw both you and George were gone, and I knew you wanted to put your brother to rest again, so…" He shrugged his shoulders.

Smeaton's look was solemn, his violin hanging at his side. He picked it up and placed it under his chin, playing a sad, somber note on behalf of George's re-burial. By the time he was done, fresh tears had rolled down my cheeks.

"Thank you," I said. "George would have enjoyed that."

We heard voices in the distance, more than likely the guards making their rounds. Their voices sounded terrified, and a small grin returned to my face.

"Same as before, My Lady?" Smeaton asked, looking towards the running guards.

"Of course," I answered. "And try to locate Jane's whereabouts while you're at it. If I can, I will come to the castle to fetch you. If not, I'll see you in a fortnight."

Smeaton looked confused. "Why so long?"

I paused. "There's still so much I need to think through, especially what I am to do with this new life I've been given... and how I can *undo* it."

He bowed. "Very well. If I shan't see you for the rest of the night, then I bid you farewell, sweet Anne." He disappeared, and it was not long before I could hear his music echoing throughout Whitehall again. Satisfied, I made my way to Rochford, Essex to pay my sister a visit.

***

I almost pitied Mary. She lived in such a small house -- a simple, little cottage, but she was also well away from the clutches of royalty. Nothing but vast fields surrounded her home. A quiet serenity to raise her children in.

I entered the premises without any problems. Everything was still. I ventured into almost every room until I came upon her quarters. She was having a very fitful sleep; she tossed and turned every so often.

I found a chair beside a window and sat down. The moonlight cast a white haze upon my ragged gown, and I frowned at it. I would have *never* allowed such beautiful damask to become so soiled had I been alive.

Mary sat up, exhaling in frustration. I remained silent as I watched on.

She came to the window with tears in her eyes as she looked up at the moon. I was surprised she had not sensed my presence in the dark corner just yet, but I preferred it that way.

"Oh my dear, sweet sister," she whispered, and I raised an eyebrow in surprise at her remark. "So many things I wished I could have said to you..."

"Then say them now," I said plainly, and she turned to me and nearly screamed, covering her mouth just in time. She backed away, hitting a table, jumped again, and collapsed onto her bed, never letting her gaze stray from the corner. She made the sign of the Holy Cross in front of herself, just as father had.

I never got up, remaining in the shadow.

"Anne?" she managed to say. "Is it your ghost that speaks to me?"

I sniffed. "If you wish it."

She put her hands to her heart and smiled as if relieved. "Oh, Anne! Sweet sister! I have not been able to sleep since your death!"

"As you should, since you never visited me in the Tower. Not even *once*. Not even a simple *letter*, Mary!" I shifted my position in the chair, but continued keeping my face in the shadows. "I never felt so abandoned until my time spent in that horrid place, so... *betrayed*!"

"Do not forget, dear sister, that you and father banished me from court, once I let it be known to you that I had married William Stafford! So please do not talk of betrayal, when it was you and father who betrayed me first."

"You did not understand the pressures of palace life, Mary! For you to be wed to a soldier --a *commoner!*-- it would have marred the appearance of our noble status! You were the sister to the queen -- you deserved *better*!"

"But I was *happy* Anne! I was *in love*! What kind of world do we live in when one has to be punished because they are happy?"

I opened my mouth but could not speak. They were very truthful words, indeed.

Mary sighed and lowered her head. "Dear sister, please don't be vexed. I would *never* abandon you. Being caught up in the king's scandal... called a whore everywhere I went... there were many things that weighed heavily on my conscience, and made me realize that to survive such a dark and trying time... it was best to *stay away* from the castle, not only for my own safety, but for the safety of our children! For who would care for my son, my daughter? And who would care for your dear Elizabeth?"

I paused, and held my breath. "Elizabeth. Is she well?"

"Of course!" she answered with a smile.

"And... how are your children?"

"Everyone is well. You should see how they play together, like the best of friends."

"They're cousins. They *should* be friends."

"Elizabeth is very strong-willed and feisty." She gave a tiny laugh. "My son and daughter are so very protective of her."

"You've done well, Mary. I should not have been so angry at you before." I leaned back in my chair, at ease again. "I am very glad she is in your care."

Mary looked at me. "Come into the light, sister. Let me see your face."

I paused. "Perhaps it is better that you don't. My appearance might drive you mad."

"If I have not gone mad already for speaking to a ghost," she replied with a knowing smirk, "I shall not get any madder."

Slowly, I got up and stood under the moonlight. I lowered my hood, and Mary tilted her head in curiosity.

"Your hair has streaks of white! It makes you look as if you've aged fifty years. Is the other side not kind to you?"

When I allowed the moonlight to grace my face, it was then that she gasped, covering her mouth again.

"Your skin is so white, Anne! You--you match the *moon*!" Mary looked as if she were about to faint as she looked at my eyes. "So red... red like *blood*! A *demon's* eyes!"

"Mary, please! Be still! You know I am no demon... but I fear I have damned myself."

She paused. "I don't understand. Damned yourself... *how*?"

"I denounced all my holy principles. My fear, grief and anger overruled my sensibility at the very *instant* before my hanging."

"Oh, *Anne*..." I could sense her disappointment in my spiritual resignation. "So many foolish sins to make at the moment of your death! How will you redeem yourself?"

I lowered my head, placing the hood back over it, and sat down. "I do not know, sister. I do not know. But I *do* know that I shall have my revenge on the king... *and* his new wife."

Mary gasped. "If it pleases you, I *must* speak on Jane's behalf."

"You know it does *not* please me, Mary. Nothing about that wench will *ever* please me."

"As the new queen, she is meek and humble, and not at all headstrong as you were. But in her humbleness, she actively seeks to restore Elizabeth to her rightful place at the throne!"

I sat up, this news most interesting. "And what about *Katharine's* daughter?"

"Jane is very family-oriented. I believe she seeks to do the same for Mary, as well."

I growled under my breath. Still, I could not ignore the fact that Jane was helping my daughter.

"She is very kind and just," my sister continued. "Spare her any tribulation you felt the need to bestow upon her, at least for your daughter's sake."

"Very well. You speak wisely, Mary. How could I doubt you?"

She grinned in relief.

"May I see her? Where is my Elizabeth?"

Mary looked taken aback. "Are you sure that is wise?"

"If you haven't feared me yet, then I'm sure my daughter will not."

Mary seemed hesitant, but she got up and beckoned me to follow. She led me to a small room where Elizabeth lay quietly in bed. I sat beside her, watching her sleep soundly.

"Have you told her about my death?" I whispered to Mary, and she shook her head.

"She asked where you were once, and I told her you had gone away for a while, but that you sent her all your love, and one day, she would see you again."

I paused. "Beautifully said, Mary. A very gentle way of describing my death without her truly knowing it."

I leaned forward and kissed Elizabeth on her forehead. She stirred and opened her eyes.

"Ma-ma," she said, sitting up to embrace me.

I sighed in joy *and* sorrow, as more fresh tears rolled down my face. "Oh my daughter," I whispered. "My beautiful, sweet child." I showered her with more kisses, and held her tight to me.

"You are so cold, ma-ma." Her tiny voice sounded like chimes.

"It is only because it is cold outside." I playfully touched the tip of her nose.

She looked into my eyes with a curious look upon her face. "What is wrong ma-ma? Are you angry?"

Angry. I sniffed at the word. So *that* was how she interpreted my looks. I thanked the heavens she did not fear me.

"Sweet Elizabeth, rest assured I am not angry at you, but at how things are in this world. I will *always* love you, for you are my bright shining star in this place of darkness."

"Will you stay with us?"

I looked at Mary standing in the doorway, her body shaking with silent sobs.

"Ma-ma has to go away again for a while. You must be strong, and always be studious, well mannered, and ever mindful of your manners. One day you *will* be Queen of England, Elizabeth, with God as my witness, you *will* be queen."

"I love you, ma-ma."

"I love you so much, Elizabeth," I cooed, rocking us back and forth. "Sleep now, my child." I tucked her under the covers. When she closed her eyes again, I placed my hand over her forehead.

"*...and forget this night... for your own safety,*" I whispered.

***

I bade Mary farewell and embraced her before I left her home. I felt comfort in knowing she had not really abandoned me, and that my daughter was safe. I decided to forego meeting with Smeaton in a fortnight in order to continue our little parlor tricks in the castle. At Whitehall Palace, I found him, telling him of my news. He was happy for me, and gave me information on Jane's whereabouts. I strayed away from the subject of torturing her, and instead focused more on Henry and the rest of his silly council and court.

Between my cruel laughter and Smeaton's joyful music echoing in the corridors of the palace at all hours of the night -- not to mention my occasional bouquets of daffodils placed around the palace at the most inconvenient and uncomfortable of times -- it was not long before the rumors of Whitehall being haunted spread like wildfire.

Henry was outraged. Every time he found one of my bouquets, he would scream in a rage and tear the flowers apart. One of his council members dared to ask him about the flowers, and Henry nearly beat the man senseless.

"These fucking *daffodils*! How I DESPISE them!" Henry spat, his nostrils flaring as he shoved the crushed flowers in the man's face. "That whoring bitch had a whole *orchard* of them at Hever Castle! They were her favorite flower, she told me, which was why she had so many of them around her home!" He paused, a crazed look in his eye. "Obviously, there are still followers of Anne around the castle, seeking to hound me to death because of my decision to have her executed!" He gripped his council member by the collar. "The culprit *must* be found and punished!"

"But, Your Majesty, where are we to look? Who are we to look *for*?"

"For a *female*, you ponce," Henry answered, letting him go. "Interrogate any woman who had ties to her. Use whatever means necessary to get to the bottom of this matter!"

"As you wish, Your Majesty." He bowed quickly and left Henry to his thoughts.

Oh no. I did not want innocent women being tortured because of me! How would I be able to stop them, if I could not come out by day? I could try to hide in the castle, but there was no guarantee I would never be discovered. I would be helpless in my slumber if I were to suddenly be found. Smeaton was also too weak during the day to spy on them, and I knew Thomas would not be able to show his face around court anymore, at least not for a good, long while.

I would have to hope that no women would be considered suspicious and tried for something they never did, before I got a chance to stop Henry's latest acts of tyranny.

***

It did not take long for members of the council to find a few alleged suspects. When I returned to the castle the next night, I found three women in the deepest, hidden bowels of the castle, where punishments were doled out to prisoners -- far away from the mirthful, oblivious, dolts of the court.

A young girl, perhaps no older than eighteen years of age, had been broken on the rack. They stripped the poor thing of all her clothing, and probably violated her before they strapped her to the horrendous device. By the looks of things, all of the joints in her shoulders, hips, knees, wrists elbows and ankles had already been dislocated, as her limbs looked abnormally longer than they should have. They left her there on the rack, dead.

Another girl, appearing to be in her twenties, had all four limbs strapped to a table. Also naked, but barely alive, her legs were spread far apart, with 'the pear of anguish' inserted into her womanhood. The pear was an extremely painful device I would not wish on anyone, it's purpose and mechanisms too ghastly to describe in great detail. She had been gagged, preventing her screams from being heard -- though I doubted she had the energy to scream anymore.

Her womanhood had been spread much farther than normal because of the device, leaving her torn, mutilated, and in a bloody pool upon the table. Despite her being gagged, I could hear her weak and labored breathing.

The final girl I knew was dead. Her pallor was as sickly as the first one. Having fell victim to the 'breast ripper', she also wound up on the Judas Cradle, which was simply a pyramid-shaped seat that her womanhood was impaled upon. They left her sitting on it for so long, she had died there on it.

I swore I never knew that Henry's mentality could ride so long alongside insanity and despotism. From his actions, it would appear he was misogynistic!

I would never be able to forgive myself for the tortures of those innocent women. They had suffered because of *my* follies. I had to figure out what to do quickly before he was angered any further and *more* innocent women would suffer Henry's wrath. Placing daffodils in Henry's presence would have to wait for a while, so I began trying other tactics.

Every crucifix and portrait in the castle I had turned upside down. Henry's own personal portraits I had facing the wall. Any minute action that would bruise his ego would surely put him in a frenzy.

Henry ordered more guards to walk the castle at night, but that did not hinder Smeaton and me at all, for no mere mortal could move about the castle as quickly as we could. He enjoyed assisting me in the most meager of tasks that easily aggravated the living world. Candles were placed upside-down in their candelabras. I was able to make the food in storage spoil quicker than normal, inviting the presence of flies and maggots. We emptied inkwells, hindering anyone from writing for bouts at a time. We scattered books from shelves, and balanced goblets and plates on each other in such a fashion that would otherwise be impossible for a normal person to duplicate.

"I feel just like a giddy schoolboy again!" Smeaton chimed, as we both had a time of ourselves in the library. We left several stacks of books piled all the way up to the *ceiling*. Let us see someone try to explain such a sight!

Then, one night, feeling in a particularly dour mood, I removed five jousting helmets from their armory, and lined them up on the dining table, along with a single daffodil placed among them. I left a note scrawled in rancid pig's blood across the floor:

Henry, see your sins.

I spread more of the blood over the helmets and the flower. Let him awaken to *that* horrid scene.

Smeaton understood the message I was leaving, and simply stood there in awe at my brazenness.

We heard several footsteps coming in our direction, so we made ourselves scarce.

Five guards happened upon the hall, and every one of them gawked at my handiwork.

"We must alert the king," one of them said, and they left in haste. It was not long before Henry returned with the guards, as well as his chancellor, Thomas Cromwell. I stared at him and sneered. He was yet another one I would have to deal with, and soon.

Henry approached the ghastly scene, covering his nose with his sleeve. Even I had to admit that I might have overdone it with the mass of pig's blood everywhere. It was slowly cascading over the table in thick, dark-red clumps, congealing in the cool atmosphere.

He read the words on the floor, looked at the daffodil and the helmets, and read the wording again. His eyes were wide, but he remained silent.

"No woman could do this," he declared. "Only a man would be so blatant and foolish."

I put my hands on my hips, irked at Henry's chauvinistic comment. I felt Smeaton patting my shoulder, trying to soothe me.

"Who *dares* to still feel sympathy for that treacherous whore and those adulterers?" he yelled to no one in particular. Henry then looked at his guards, his stare so primal, I thought he would strike every one of them.

"Why are you not doing your jobs?!" he demanded. "I want you to catch this culprit, or it will be *your heads* representing those helmets!"

They bowed and quickly ran off once more.

Try as they might, no one would find the 'culprits'. *Ever.*

***

Smeaton and I kept a low profile afterwards, keeping our mischievousness to a minimum. I left him in charge of ghostly disturbances for a while, requesting him to play expressly for the king as much as possible and as close to Henry as he could, while I kept to myself for a time. I did not intend to leave anyone in the clear for long. I needed to regroup my thoughts once again.

Despite it all, nothing impeded the wedding of Henry and Jane. On the day of the event, Thomas and I invited ourselves, while I cloaked the two of us in a sort of invisibility spell, which didn't take me long to learn. Basically, it was all a simple task of mind over matter.

By it being daytime, I was very drained and weak, but Thomas kept me sheltered with a generous sized cloak he had a servant make for me. Despite us going about unseen, Thomas kept us towards the back of the crowds.

Even he had a bit of mischievousness in him, swiping food from plates as he grew hungry throughout the day, leaving those hapless victims of his actions wondering where their food had disappeared to.

Henry never looked so happy. He even looked *happier* than when he and I were married! I seethed at their bliss, and hissed under my breath. Thomas cast a wary glance at me.

"You don't… still love him… *do* you?"

"I have no more love for him than I have for Cromwell. He too, is an enemy that won't go unpunished."

Thomas seemed relieved to hear that.

I refused to let the whole day go by without giving *some* sort of warning. Amongst the colorfully coordinated red and white bouquets placed throughout the hall, I produced several yellow daffodils in each one. After everyone was finished with their daft wedding dances and settled down to eat, Henry noticed the flowers, and it looked like he was about to have a mental breakdown right then and there. Not wanting to put on a show of hysterics in front of Jane, especially on what was supposed to be a joyous occasion, he called a few of his servers to him, telling them to remove every single daffodil in sight. Before long, Henry also made a silly decree that anyone bringing in *any* yellow flowers into the castle, or had one about their person, would be put in the stocks for three days.

When the sun had set, I did not have the strength to go about my nightly antics. Forcing myself to remain 'awake' during the day took a toll on me. I rested that night and into the following day, and did not awaken until nightfall. Even then, I was losing my lust for revenge again. These frequent changes in my mood were annoying, keeping me unfocused, and I knew part of the reason I had them was because of this new un-life I was leading. This duality in my persona had me unsure, yet certain, at peace, but still disturbed. I wished I knew exactly what dark forces caused me to have this *thing*, this strange affliction that made me part human and part demon. I wanted to confront it, so I could die again. I had been so afraid of death before, but now, it seemed more of a refuge than something to fear. This un-life I led was nothing more but a cruel mockery than anything else. Perhaps Thomas was on to something when he was working on his literary project.

He was not around when I awoke, which was all the more better for me. I was not in much of a talkative mood again, for my mind was spinning with too many thoughts.

No matter how much I tortured those around me, life was still moving on, and moving on *without me*.

This un-life would not give me the chance to simply pick up where I left off, and in the barest of truths, I had left off being *dead*. My death was my finale. The final exit. My existence had ceased to be. There was nothing for me to go back to, because my time on earth was finished.

Wanting revenge would also gain me nothing in the end. Once I *had* exacted my vengeance, what then? Now it seemed like a frivolous pastime for the bored and shiftless -- and I knew I was neither!

Revenge also had its repercussions. It already cost a few innocent people their lives. I did not need such guilt on my head, but it was much too late now.

Thomas entered the room, surprised to see me.

"Anne. I had thought you'd be long gone by now."

I gave a half smile, and looked out of the window.

He walked over to me and put a hand on my shoulder. "What's troubling you? As if I need to ask."

I faced him head-on, my look full of resolve. "I want you to kill me, Thomas Wyatt."

He blinked in disbelief. "Come again?"

"I want you to kill me," I repeated. "I think I am done with this twisted life of mine."

He sniffed. "Deliver you into the hands of death -- for a *second* time? No, I do not think I could stomach that. Seeing you die once was enough. I haven't the heart nor the strength to see you die *again*, much less commit the act of killing you *myself*."

"If *I* had the will to do it, I'd have done it already. But for some strange reason, I cannot."

"It takes a very brave and very fearless person to commit suicide, Anne. Also one who believes, yet does not care that they'll go straight to hell for their actions."

"I'm already in hell, Thomas. Hell is all around us. People are just too blind to see it. And those who *do* see have not the ability to change it."

Thomas took my hands. "Anne, I know you can get a little morose at times, but this is not the Anne I came to know and love. Where is that unquenchable fire for life? Those passions insatiable?" He stood close to me, our foreheads almost touching. "That lust for all things forbidden?"

"*That* was not part of your poem, Thomas," I whispered.

"I know," he whispered back, and our lips met once more.

Oh, such sweet sin! How I yearned to do unspeakable things to him! His kisses were deep, our tongues entwined in a sensual frenzy.

"Anne," he whispered. "I've missed you so much... and how I've missed the feeling of being inside of you..."

He led us backwards towards the bed. I could feel the warmth of his body heat rising, while mine could not reciprocate.

I was on my back before I knew it, and he raised my gown, his warm hand running down the length of my dead-cold thigh.

"Sweet Anne," he whispered, his kisses traveling down my chest. "I want to make love to you, I want things to be like how they were before…"

I broke away from him, and sat up, trying to catch my breath.

"What are we doing, Thomas? This is nonsense! We are living in the past! Do you not see the *thing* you are trying to love?"

Thomas was getting very flustered until he got a sudden revelation. He unbuttoned his shirt halfway, and leaned his neck towards me.

"Do what you did to me before, then," he said firmly. "If I can't be like you, then at least I'll die in your arms."

Spoken like a true poet.

I leaned forward, and bit into him as gently as I could. His blood was rich and warm in my mouth, and while I suckled his neck, I could feel the pulse of his body, the thrum of his life entering me. It felt vibrant, shocking… *alive*. All the things I was not.

I wondered if I really could make him like me, but I could not subject him to this half-life. I also did not want to kill him accidentally.

I drank from him until it sufficed me, then I rolled him off to my side, where he stayed, unmoving. He was not dead, only very weak. Moreover, his pep talk encouraged me to finish up my agenda once more.

***

In the forthcoming days, I decided to space out the times in which I would 'haunt' Whitehall. I did not want our hauntings to be so frequent, that the living would soon grow used to it. Sometimes, I would even go a month before Smeaton or I would do something to disconcert everyone again.

After some time, if I did not feel like doing the haunting myself, I would simply summon up a bevy of un-living creatures to roam the cemetery grounds. When the common folk noticed my morbid creations moving about at night, it caused such a disturbance throughout the towns that both England and my living-dead regiments were fast becoming known as, *Henry's Lands of the Dead*, *The King's Unquiet Souls*, or worse, *Henry's Dead Devils*. I never laughed so much in my lifetime.

Henry did not appreciate such dubious titles, and again tried making decrees stating that using such titles were treasonous and punishable by public humiliation in the pillory. Even so, most folks never bothered to heed them.

Christmastide was a low-spirited time for everyone. With Henry's religious laws in effect, the usual atmosphere at this time of year seemed droll, less merry. It was the perfect time to start up my dark revelry again.

I caught one unsuspecting guard in a corridor, and drained him completely of his life's essence, leaving him there on the spot for someone else to find. Smeaton did the more annoying tasks; making nearby objects disappear and reappear elsewhere -- goblets of wine people might have been drinking from, especially -- causing them to doubt their own sanity. Before the night was through, murmuring was heard amongst the people about 'strange, abnormal things' happening again. Word had gotten around to Henry, and he was *not* amused.

Good.

My grand gift to the king that evening was an entire corridor's floor *carpeted* with daffodils, splattered in blood. All his portraits in that hallway had the words, *Henry, the adulterer* scrawled across them. When he came upon the scene, I was sure his scream could have been heard throughout the entire palace. Jane was kept away from the area, unfortunately. Such a shame. It would have been nice to see the expression of terror mar her pretty, demure face.

I had lain low again for a few more months, until Smeaton gave me news of Jane being with child. I was suddenly filled with a dread that had me at ill ease. Although Jane had kept her word concerning restoring Elizabeth to her rightful place, her 'place' would still be after Jane's own child, *and* Katharine's. That of course, was Henry's doing, and was to be expected, *especially* if she gave birth to a son.

My desire to torment her, to make her lose the child, was great. As she came closer and closer to term, my worry increased. Henry showered her with love and affection, giving Jane whatever her heart desired, and it made me *sick*. I saw the vast differences in how he treated her compared to me, and it angered me knowing he caused me to miscarry his son, all because of Henry wenching with *her* whilst I was pregnant.

One night, I hurled a vase of flowers, smashing it against a wall and right beside his head as he stood in her chambers, cooing over her large, rounding belly. That had caused them both to tremble in fear, and Henry ordered two guards to watch over their chambers for the rest of the night. How long would it take for him to realize that you cannot order an army of the living to fight against one of the dead?

Katharine's daughter, Mary, had gotten word of the occasional hauntings. How I loathed her so. With her still being alive, she still had a chance at being queen before my Elizabeth. She prayed frequently, often speaking as if she were talking to her mother. My one bane was that I could not torment her, no matter how much I tried. It was as if something protected her from my evil doings. It might have been God himself.

Another night, when I decided to try to give Jane another scare, I noticed the floor of her chamber doorway was completely lined with *pomegranates*. I cringed in surprise. It looked like I was not the only one roaming the palace's corridors.

Katharine was here, too.

She made sure to keep out of my sight. She was *protecting* Jane, as well as her daughter. And either Henry did not notice the pomegranates, or did not care, because he never made a fuss of seeing them. It only angered me more.

Every night I tried to pay Jane a 'visit', the pomegranates would appear. I decided to ignore them one time, entering Jane's room, anyway. The moment I did, I was thrown back with such a force; I hit the wall in the hallway, crashing into a suit of decorative armor. The crash made such a commotion, footsteps fast approached. I escaped before anyone arrived.

Jane could not explain how her chamber doors had opened by themselves, nor why the armor fell in the hallway. After that incident, Henry had her sleeping in his own chambers.

That damned Katharine!

Smeaton was able to see her, whereas, for some strange reason, I could not. He told me of Katharine's occasional wanderings, silent and vigilant, dressed in all black, not disturbing anyone, only keeping a sort of 'watch' over things. He too, believed Mary's prayers were secret requests to her mother to protect herself and Jane from the 'malicious evildoings' that happened occasionally at the palace.

Elizabeth seemed unaffected either way by the goings-on. Perhaps she even sensed I was nearby, as one time I caught her out of bed, walking the halls, as if she was looking for something. However, Mary -- of all people -- kindly led her back to her bedroom. I was shocked to see that she showed concern for my daughter, or perhaps she merely did it out of courtesy.

Another night, I received a message that was expressly meant for me. On an empty table in the dining hall, I spotted a large pile of pomegranates. As I approached them, I noticed some feathers underneath them.

Those feathers belonged to a falcon. Its dead body protruded from underneath the pile; its blank eye staring up at me.

This sign had meant Katharine's triumph over me. Katharine's symbol was the pomegranate, as the falcon was my own. I screamed in frustration, smacking the pile of pomegranates and the dead bird onto the floor.

As I composed myself, I paused in sudden revelation. I now saw that what happened to me was the *exact* same thing that had happened to Katharine. Henry betrayed me by seeing Jane behind my back. Henry had betrayed Katharine by seeing *me* behind hers! Oh, how ugly history could be in repeating itself!

In addition, as much as I hated to admit it, Katharine had been right all along. When I was her lady-in-waiting, and she suspected Henry of courting me, she warned me of Henry's promiscuousness and stated he would eventually tire of me. In my own arrogance, I ignored her words, and now, I realized that it was a dark omen all along.

I put a hand to my forehead in despair. I did not want to cry, so I took a deep breath. As I turned to leave, I finally saw Katharine for the first time.

She was standing at the opposite end of the room, watching me, not saying a word. Her face was stern and unreadable. I gasped in surprise.

"All hail Anne, the scandal of Christendom!" she said with a dead cold glare, and disappeared.

I gave a noise of annoyance. How *dare* she say such a thing to me!

I never saw her again, however. Even so, Smeaton told me she was still roaming Whitehall, and would continue to do so, as long as I roamed there.

Well, if Katharine wanted to stay, then fine by me. She could haunt her part of the castle, and I would haunt *mine*. There was plenty of room for *all* of us, and *I* had no intention of leaving!

Chapter Five

Another religious revolt had risen out of Henry declaring himself head of the Church of England, and the reformation that came afterward. Coined *The Pilgrimage of Grace*, it was born of simple townsfolk and commoners, aghast at how their faith and beliefs had been stripped from them. Why were politics and religion *always* the two main reasons of great conflict between men?

Tension, ire, frustrations and mistrust were abounding between both sides, and Henry would not let the rebellion's actions go unpunished. He led them to believe that he had reconciled and understood their reason for their revolt, and led them right into his trap of false trust. They thought that they would be able to disband in peace, but Henry had hundreds of men from the rebellion slain all over England's lands -- as well as *anyone* with close ties to it. In the end, the heads of the leaders were wedged onto lances and placed in prominent areas around the castle for all to see; a horrid, ghastly reminder not only of Henry's autocracy, but also of the repercussions one would face in defiance of the king. The heads remained out in the elements for so long, the ravens made a feast of their rotting carrion.

Alas, once more, England's rolling green hills were washed in red.

And now, I was no longer the only one haunting the lands at night. Several women were mourning the loss of their loved ones; wives and daughters still clutching the bodies of their hung husbands and fathers, as the dead men's ghosts could do nothing but watch them grieve. Eventually, more bodies were buried in new potter's fields, silent vigils held over many graves.

In the distance, I saw several candle lights over the lands, and heard the wailing of many females. Sometimes I even joined them in their lamentations. It looked as if death could be so very cruel. It came anytime, anywhere, and took anyone at any age. Death cared not if you were young or old, rich or poor. It seemed such an unrelenting thing. Although we know death is a part of life, it's that part of life that everyone wishes they could do without. In its arms, mortality is so very tenuous.

Several times, I tried praying to God, but again, it appeared as if my prayers went unheard. After the horrid things I had said to Him, I doubted He would listen anymore.

In the meantime, Jane's ladies-in-waiting were very doting. It still disgusted me seeing Henry being just as devoted. I knew several things were not in my favor when I was crowned queen, as I knew how supportive the people were to Katharine as well as to Jane. Sometimes, I wondered if I was simply born under an unlucky star. For some reason, Fate deemed it right to bestow on me such a doomed life.

I still had a chance to reign, though, and it would be through *Elizabeth*. I would never, *ever* give up on that.

Then, came the moment everyone was waiting for. It was time for Jane to bring another life into the world. Another heir to the throne.

Henry called on his physicians, and her chambers bustled with excitement as well as anxiousness. Her ladies ran back and forth with bloody sheets and towels in their hands. Cromwell kept the king constantly updated as to Jane's progress. So far, things were not faring well. She was having trouble bringing the baby forth, and I smiled in nefarious anticipation.

I wandered into Henry's study, where he sat, dazed and in a sort of shock. Every time Cromwell approached with gloomy news, it seemed that Henry was sinking more and more into depression. It was a possibility that the baby would have to be cut out of Jane, or risk losing both her *and* the child. Katharine's daughter faithfully remained by Jane's side throughout the whole ordeal.

Henry was anguished. He gripped his hair and paced the room after Cromwell's last announcement.

"Don't take her from me God, please," he pleaded. "Let Jane live…"

"Poor, pretty Jane," I mocked. Henry whipped around, and saw me sitting at his table. My hood well over my head and hiding my face. He could not see me outright.

"What business have you here, woman?" he snapped. "If you bring no good news, I order you to leave at once!"

"You can't order me around," I said snidely. "You lost your right long ago."

He approached me, but paused in his tracks. "Your voice," he said to himself, trying to get a better look at me.

"Your Majesty," I heard Cromwell say quickly before he entered the room. When Henry turned to acknowledge him, Cromwell bowed before saying she had finally delivered.

Before he rushed out of the room, he turned back to look at me, but I had already gone.

***

To my surprise and dread, Henry had finally gotten his wish. Jane had given birth to a boy, Edward, and she made Mary his Godmother. Edward's christening ceremony was joyous and lavish. Everyone was so elated at the outcome! I seethed in my own jealousy, and Katharine took great pains not to allow me to spoil the next few days. I do believe Mary somehow knew her mother's spirit was always nearby -- whenever Katharine was within a few paces of her daughter, Mary would secretly smile.

These colossal events did little for Jane's health, however. The birthing took a great toll on her, and she had barely gotten any rest afterwards. Only days later, she came down with a fever that Henry's physicians could do little to fix. Bleeding her did her no good, and she fell more and more into sickness. Henry catered to her every whim again, giving Jane whatever she wished for. She had odd cravings for wine and sweets, and so she received them without question.

A few times, I desired to enter her chambers, but Katharine remained firm and vigilant. Any mischievous intentions on my part were immediately counterattacked. Whatever I tried to throw in anger, was reflected right back at me. Even Smeaton could do nothing to upset Jane or the baby, although Smeaton took care to stay out of Katharine's path in any case.

Henry stayed by Jane's bedside constantly. It was as if the whole kingdom held their breath, wondering and worrying whether she would survive. Jane had been the light in everyone's world, Henry's especially; as he made sure it was well known to everyone.

Jane's ladies continued to watch over her very carefully, and Mary visited her very often, with Katharine's spirit by her side. It was to Mary's shock that Jane managed to speak to her when they were alone.

"I see your mother... she is here with us," she said, giving a weak smile.

Mary's eyes widened as she held Jane's hand. "Is she *really*?"

Jane nodded slowly. "She is smiling, and stroking your hair. She is *so* proud of you."

Mary's eyes welled with tears as she held Jane's hand tighter. "I could feel her watching over us, and over you. I *knew* she would."

"She tells you to always stay strong." Jane took a deep breath and tried to reposition herself in her bed. "You have the spirit of your grandmother and mother combined. I see it in your eyes. You'll never disappoint her."

Mary smiled, as I grimaced.

"You're a good girl, Mary. Your mother raised a beautiful, resilient, young woman. You have a bright future ahead of you."

In the days to come, Jane had gotten so weak to the point where she could not even speak anymore. The day Henry had been dreading the most had finally come.

Jane had died barely within two weeks of giving birth to their son. The physicians claimed it was childbed fever, a very common ailment amongst women in those days.

There were no words descriptive enough to explain Henry's mental state after Jane's death. It might have been deep grief, or it might have been a bout of insanity, but no one was able to talk any sense into Henry. Jane's body was laid to rest at a tomb in Windsor Castle, which Henry had been building for himself. He visited her constantly, and talked with her of his woes, wishing he could be where she was. When he was not visiting her, he would shut himself away from the palace, not coming out for days at a time, except to visit her tomb again. He did not shave or bathe, and demanded that no one bother him for anything at all, for he was in mourning, and had no idea when he would ever stop.

And to think, poor Jane never got the chance to experience the one event *I* did.

Her own coronation.

I had heard it was to be an extremely lavish one, *much* more extravagant than mine had been. Henry went through great lengths to show her how much he loved her, and now his efforts had been wasted. However, it was rumored he was waiting to see if Jane would bear him a son first *before* he paraded her around, which, to me, showed a hint of his own selfishness and doubt. But no matter. His new queen was dead.

I gave a little grin of conceit.

As the king continued his period of mourning, I saw this as the start of yet another perfect opportunity to torture Henry, and I would do it *very* well.

I began by leaving Jane's wedding gown neatly laid out on Henry's bed. When he retired to his chambers for the night, I really thought I had driven him *over* the brink of madness. He screamed, cried, and clutched her gown as his guards could do nothing but watch on. For the next two days afterwards, he stayed in his room, lying in bed, still clutching the gown, staring off into a place where no one could reach him. By the second night, he got some radical notion that her wedding dress on his bed was a sign that maybe Jane was *not* dead, and made a mad dash to her resting place. He demanded several groundsmen to open her tomb, hoping she had not been buried alive. Having no choice but to obey his grim and macabre command, they opened her marble casket and were welcomed with the undeniable stench of decay. Henry dared not peer into the dark sepulcher, only collapsed to his knees at her crypt and wailed in agony, his futile hopes crushed in that instant.

Rumors about the king going insane were increasing. His council members were making their best effort to squelch such remarks. The kingdom had no king, so long as he kept going about his morbid routine. So, in the king's absence, his advisors did their best to keep the peace.

Cromwell seemed to gain a smug delight in taking over while Henry grieved, though some appeared not to approve of it, believing he was overreaching himself. I happened upon his studies one evening, finding him working on some very important papers. It did not matter what they were to me; the fact was that he was alone, and at my disposal.

I brought a small army of undead soldiers into the castle with me. Nothing enormous; four would suffice my plan. They shuffled and dragged themselves down the dimly lit corridors to Cromwell's study, with me in the lead. I entered without warning, requesting my army to stay outside his door for the moment. I kept a good distance away from his desk at first, simply waiting for him to sense my presence.

Cromwell looked up from his papers, giving me an odd stare.

"Woman, what is the meaning of this interruption? Should I know you?"

I lowered my hood. He still seemed perplexed, but my appearance *did* unnerve him. Slowly Cromwell stood, not saying a word.

"Speak, woman," he said firmly, "Before I have my guards arrest you."

"On what grounds?" I asked. "Besides, you already had me arrested *once*."

Still not knowing what to make of his situation, I approached his desk with blinding speed. He gasped and jumped back.

"How did you do that?" His voice trembled. "What un-holiness is this?"

The candlelight cast a dull orange reflection off my white skin, as his eyes widened in terror while he stared into my own.

"It can't be..." he whispered, backing away from his desk. "Boleyn? No -- this is *impossible*! You were *executed*!"

With a thought, I commanded my troops to enter his study. He looked past me, watching my shambling dead army march in. Once he realized that there was no breath within those walking corpses, did Cromwell scream.

"It is time for justice, you avaricious ponce," I hissed, descending upon him, fangs bared.

***

One of my undead army men snatched a black hood off of Cromwell's head. He was unconscious, so I slapped him awake. He gasped, shaking his head, and then looked around himself.

Cromwell stood on the scaffold, his neck in the hangman's noose. Hands tied behind his back, he gave pathetic, whiny noises of fear as the crowd around the gallows was nothing more but a sea of the dead, the majority of them the ones who died during the bloody onslaught caused by the Pilgrimage. The moonlight cast a pale, grisly glow over the worm-infested crowd as I now stood in the center of them, smiling at him, my arms folded.

"How does it feel, Cromwell?" I called out. "To be judged and tried for crimes you never committed?" I gave a mock gesture of surprise by covering my mouth. "But then again, I stand corrected, don't I? Aren't you partly responsible for all these innocent lives lost?" I gestured to the ghoulish group around me. "So tell me, *what does it feel like?*"

"Let me go!" he cried out, and another one of my soldiers tightened the noose around his neck.

Irked, I appeared before him, scaring the daylights out of him yet again.

"You were a witch all along! Henry's marriage to you *was* born out of sorcery!"

"You fool," I hissed. "I was no witch *then*... not that it matters now."

Through his torn shirt, I glanced at the base of his neck and the two marks I left there earlier. I ripped the shirt further, pressed my index finger against the wounds, and callously wiped off a trickle of blood that lingered there. He winced in pain as I licked my finger next, frowning at him as I did so.

"I do not like how you taste." I frowned, and spat in his face. Cromwell flinched in disgust as a mixture of his blood and my saliva ran down his cheek.

I turned my back to him, and, while not even looking, waved at a third soldier to release the hatch as I walked down the scaffold's rickety steps.

The hatch dropped, and Cromwell swung. However, Cromwell was tough, and a mercenary in his youth, so I heard. He would not give up without a fight.

I let him writhe, thrash, and sway wildly by his neck until he was just near the brink of death -- then the soldier who released the hatch produced a knife from his tattered, fraying doublet. He cut the noose, and Cromwell dropped through the hatch, falling to the ground with a thud.

My army men clambered down the steps, walked under the scaffolding, and dragged Cromwell out from underneath it. I stood over him, peering down at his terrified face.

"Be lucky I didn't have you cropped at the neck," I said, giving an evil grin. "But I need not worry; you'll get yours in due time."

I left him there among the moldering crowd that began to circle him. I cared not what they did to him, as his screams echoed throughout the Tower grounds, and well into the night.

***

The great hall now desolate and empty, I took a seat upon the king's throne, running my hands over the mahogany armrests. I gazed out into the empty room, imagining it filled with the laughter, mirth and merriment of those who came to court, dressed in their finest damask or satin, and lively music being played by my beloved Smeaton, as young ladies spun and danced with their gentlemen. Plentiful food and wine sat before me. I closed my eyes and practically heard the noises ringing in my ears, smell the scents of meats and cheeses, taste the wine upon my lips...

I gripped the armrests, trying to cling onto those not-so-distant memories, willing it all to appear before me once more. I gripped them so hard; they began to crack in my clutches. The noise resounded throughout the chamber, breaking my concentration, and I opened my eyes, surrounded by the cold, dismal emptiness of the hall once more.

I began to sob, and hugged myself tightly, wanting to hold in my sorrow. I breathed deeply, calmed myself down, and *laughed* instead, listening to my voice as it echoed throughout the castle.

"*LONG LIVE THE QUEEN!*"

Chapter Six

Nights later, I discovered through Smeaton that Cromwell had been sent to bedlam for a while. Henry refused to believe his rants about seeing the king's second wife resurrected as some vile, demonic creature, and the barrage of the dead that surrounded him during his near-hanging. Henry and some of his council members decided that Cromwell had become too stressed by his duties to the king, and sought a way to 'alleviate' himself of those stresses by trying to hang himself. I could not have been more happier at hearing this.

Thomas laughed when I passed the news to him.

"I never liked that bastard anyway," he said. "Good riddance to bad rubbish. Right, Anne?" He rubbed the back of his hair, giving me a half-grin.

I chuckled to myself, smiling at him. But then, my smile wavered. I could tell something was on his mind.

"What is it Thomas?" I asked. He slowly walked away from me, his arms crossed.

"I want to make a petition to the king," he replied. "I want to ask for his forgiveness and see if I can get reinstated back into the Privy Council."

My jaw dropped in shock. "Are you *mad*? Why return to the place that was so ready to *condemn* you? You're like a sheep willingly entering the wolf's lair!"

"Ah, but this sheep can keep you well informed of the wolf's doings." He raised his eyebrow at me. "It might make things easier for you if I can tell you what is happening during the day, while you are resting here. I know how going about in the daytime is a huge exertion on you -- although I know of *some* exertions you didn't mind going through…" He grabbed me by my waist and grinned. I rolled my eyes, pushing his hands down and away.

"You have *no* idea what you would be getting into, Thomas. Besides, if I made you like me, then you'd defeat your own plans to assist me."

He paused, shaking his head in annoyance. "Alas, the grief I bring upon myself!"

***

Thomas sent word to the king, asking for an audience with him. Word came back to Thomas a few days later, the king accepting his request. Thomas wore his finest attire before heading off to the palace, and I kissed him as if I would never see him again. Henry was so unpredictable, so changeable; many knew that what he said was law, and that his law was never a permanent thing. One had to learn to tread very lightly around him, as he made many, *many*, empty promises. Thomas may have been free now, but Henry could charge him with some other far-fetched offense later. I prayed no such situation would ever come to pass.

Thomas had been gone for one… two… three whole days. I did not like the feel of things by then, so on the forth night, I made my way to Whitehall. I took my time this go 'round, enjoying the night and its splendors. This was one thing I always enjoyed, and despite my predicament, I cast my worries aside to enjoy the cool air, the light of the moon, and all the nightly sounds that went with it.

Up ahead on the dirt road I traveled on, I could hear a small child crying under a huge oak tree. I quickened my pace, only to find a little boy sitting cross-legged on the grass.

"I want my ma-ma," he said between weeping.

"Oh, dear child! How did you get to be out here so late at night?" I asked, stooping down to get closer to him.

"Where's my ma-ma?" he asked.

"Do you live near here? Come with me, and we will find your home. Do not worry. You'll be safe with me."

I reached forward to pick him up and gasped when my arms went right through him.

He was a ghost.

I quickly stood up and stared at the poor boy.

"Ma-ma! I want my ma-ma!" he said, weeping harder.

"Child! Can you not hear me? Speak to me!"

For some reason, the child never responded. I found this so strange. Perhaps there were things about the land of the dead that were well beyond my knowledge. I could see Smeaton, but I never saw Katharine, save for that one time. Moreover, I could see this child before me, but it appeared as if he could not see or hear *me*. Being undead could drive one mad if one let it.

As I looked past the oak, I had a sneaking suspicion as to why this child's ghost still haunted this world. A potter's field lay not too far ahead. He may have been buried there, and his mother might have been somewhere in this field as well. Or *not*.

I sighed, hating to leave this child alone, but I had no way of communicating with him. I figured with the abilities I had, I might have been able to do *something* for him, but alas, no.

Continuing onward, my mood was getting dour. I wondered what happened to Thomas, so I picked up the pace, arriving at Whitehall in no time.

I cloaked myself in another invisibility spell again, so I could walk amongst the people of court, and not worry about skulking around.

The revelry was at a minimum. There was not even any music playing, or dancing. Court was abuzz with voices, and the talk was still about the king and his continued absence from his kingdom. It made me wonder about Thomas' petition, and I hoped the King's agreement to see him was not a trick. Besides, it had been well over a year now, since my death, and Thomas *should* have been in good standing with the king once more, especially since he was cleared of all charges.

"My Lady," a voice came to my right, and I turned.

"Smeaton," I said, smiling, almost forgetting I was unable embrace him. "Court looks so *empty* these days."

"As it should. The king is still in a bad state. He wanders about on occasion, but never converses with anyone. He still goes to Jane's tomb and talks to her as if she is alive. If the king does not quit his antics, the council might have to take more drastic measures with keeping the kingdom in order... which might include *replacing* the king."

"They can *do* that?"

"It appears so, but I'm not sure. You know I don't know about such things."

I paused. "Who is keeping order now, since Cromwell is still in bedlam?"

"As far as I can tell, the entire council."

I caught a glimpse of Henry walking through the crowds in the distance. The Duke of Suffolk and a few other members of the Privy Council followed after him.

"I'll see you soon," I told Smeaton, taking off after them.

They entered one of Henry's private chambers, one that even I had not known of when I was queen. Charles -- the *Duke* -- shut the door just moments after I rushed in.

"Gentlemen," Henry started. "I've called you here because I have questions. I keep hearing malicious talk of my ill mental health, as well as more of that silly nonsense about Whitehall being haunted."

"May I speak?" Charles asked. Henry gestured for him to proceed. "It seems, Your Majesty, that the good people of England are simply worried about Your Highness. It has been over two weeks now, and Your Majesty shows no signs of being... a *king*."

"Aren't kings allowed to grieve for their dead queens?" Henry yelled.

"What the Duke is saying, Your Majesty, is that the kingdom needs its king, if only to let his people know that all is well with him," said one of the councilmen.

"We know your loss was very great," said another. "But you must not dwell in such dark memories for so long. You must push onward, My Lord, for yourself, as well as for the good of all."

Henry sat down in a chair, paused for a moment, and nodded. I could practically feel the tension in the air lift after his agreement with them.

"Now, what of these silly superstitions about *ghosts* in Whitehall?" Henry continued. "Why are such things being spoken of, as if they exist? *I* say it is a malevolent prankster, trying to humiliate me! Why has this prankster not been caught?"

"How can such a prankster be caught if he seems to be in more than one place at any given time?" Charles asked.

Henry's eyes widened in anger and he jumped up. "Then it's *obvious* that there's *more than one of them*!" He smacked Charles in the back of his head. "Ponce!"

I snickered and covered my mouth, not wanting them to hear me.

"What of the guard that was found nearly dead?"

"Ah, Anthony," said a third council member. "He goes about the palace in a sort of delirium. He still hasn't strayed from his story that a woman -- not a wild animal -- bit him."

I gasped. That guard... I thought I had drained him completely of all his blood! And to hear he survived... I rubbed my chin, deep in thought.

Henry looked taken aback. "A *woman*? Was he *drunk* when he spoke of this? What did the physicians say?"

"That he was lucky to still be alive when he was found," the council member continued. "Anthony may talk as if he is out of his mind, but otherwise, he is harmless."

"I ought to send him to bedlam with Cromwell," Henry growled. No one said a word.

"There have still been reports of a strange woman being seen at all times of night," Charles said, giving a long pause as if reluctant to say his next sentence. "Some believe it is the ghost of Anne Boleyn."

"Don't you *dare* speak her name aloud again!" Henry bellowed. "I do not wish to hear it!" He gave a huge sigh. "Why is it always a *woman*?" Henry sneered at them and sat down again. "I saw such a strange woman as well, the same day that Jane gave birth to our son. 'Poor, pretty, Jane,' she said to me. Then Cromwell came into the room to tell me the good news of our son's delivery, and the woman simply... vanished."

The council members all looked at each other in wonder.

"Plus, there's talk of a woman's laughter in the dead of night, and that infernal violin that plays at all times! Even *I* hear such noises, and it's driving me *insane*!"

"But, Your Majesty, if you hear them as well--" Suffolk started.

"That's still no excuse to believe they are *ghosts*," Henry interrupted. "Between Cromwell going mad and seeing the dead, and those damned daffodils appearing everywhere, paintings defiled with blood -- *pig's* blood, even! Those bloody helmets in the hall, rumors of that bitch's alleged ghost running about Whitehall -- they are *pranks* that have gone on for *far* too long! I want them *stopped*, gentlemen, and I want those responsible *punished*! They have tortured me, and they have tortured my beloved Jane. They know of my chambers, and they know what angers me! Some have even had the audacity to believe it *was* who you mentioned." He looked over to Charles.

The Duke shifted his position slightly, and kept looking around the room.

"Charles!" Henry eyed him carefully. "What is the matter?"

"I can't quite help feeling, Your Majesty, that something is *watching* us."

Damn Charles to hell!

The rest of the men fell silent, looking around the room as well. They kept passing over the corner in which I stood, not sure where to pinpoint the cause for their anxiety.

"Come, come, gentlemen! We should be beyond the age of superstitions and ghosts. I want those culprits found, and for this silliness to end *immediately*."

The council members bowed at the king before leaving, and as Charles opened the door, I laughed at them before running out. All the men stumbled backward, looking at each other, not knowing what to believe as they mumbled amongst themselves.

***

I walked down the hallway, slowly making my way back to court, as I pondered what on earth could have happened to Thomas. I had hoped that little council meeting might have given me a clue to his whereabouts.

Henry and the Duke passed me while the other council members took their leave of them. On that note, I decided to follow the two of them... just in case.

"What of Sir Thomas Wyatt?" Henry asked him, and my heart leapt in anticipation. "Is he ready to come back to council?"

"He hasn't changed much in my opinion," Charles answered, sounding stern. "He still gambles, whores, and drinks. The first night he came back to court, I caught him whoring with one of Jane's former ladies-in-waiting. But, despite it all, he continues to swear fealty to My Lord."

Henry sniffed and grinned. "Sounds like Thomas all the way." He laughed, and clapped the Duke on his back. "Very well, you can release him from the pillory." Henry paused, thinking it over. "...Whenever you feel ready."

***

I made my way down to the dungeons, where I knew they were

keeping Thomas. The pillory! Of all things! I had a mind to leave him there, for all the good it did him! Whoring already, and with one of Jane's former ladies! I gave a noise of annoyance. *Men!*

This area of the castle was always so rank with foul odors. Between the unclean bodies, human waste, spilt blood, and the bevy of rats eating scraps of leftover, rotted food -- with no sort of ventilation down here, it was enough to make anyone sick with nausea.

The yellowish-orange glow from the torches lighting the dungeons danced and flickered against the huge, cobble-stoned walls, creating looming, ominous shadows in my wake. The flooring was littered with dirty straw. I nearly stepped on a family of rats and their droppings as I hurried on.

"Thomas," I whispered, peering into the prison doors. "Thomas!"

It would not be easy to recognize him if I could not see his face. Every prisoner down here looked the same; filthy with grime, their clothing just as bad, unwashed and bedraggled, and streaked with a combination of dirt and blood, or worse, depending on the type of torture they were given.

I kept calling his name. Finally, I heard him respond. I peeked through the tiny window of his solid, wooden door, and saw him on his knees, his head and hands bound between two locked wooden boards so he could not escape. He was trying to rest the awkward entrapment on a short pedestal. No other parts of his body were restrained. He had been free to move about in his cell.

"Anne!" He tried getting up, but with some difficulty. The pillory was not exactly lightweight. When he stood, he stumbled his way to the door. "It's so good to see you, my love!"

"If you weren't already being punished, I'd smack you," I snapped. "Three days in court and you're already whoring."

His face grew red underneath the filth that coated his face. "I thought of *you* all the while, though!"

"Simpleton!" I hissed. "The Duke should leave you there in your misery!"

"Anne, what was I to do? The king decided to accept me back... after I did a bit of penance. I just wanted to celebrate!"

I put a hand to my forehead. "Nevertheless, I can't let you out.

Charles will. Just pray he does it soon. From the looks of it, he doesn't have to rush."

He swallowed as he gave me a nervous look.

I sniffed. "If you lie with the dogs, you'll wake up with fleas, Thomas," I said, giving him a smirk as I walked away.

***

Thomas spent one more day in the pillory before the Duke came to release him.

"Your countenance is spotty at best," he started. "Straighten up your act, Wyatt. I will be keeping an eye on you. You'll report to the king in two days." Charles looked him up and down. "That should give you enough time to... *clean up*, and recuperate."

Thomas bowed his head, and the Duke left Thomas to leave the dungeons on his own accord. I came out of hiding to get a good look at his face. That impish twinkle was still there.

"Weren't you terrified?" I asked him.

He hunched his shoulders, and then winced. There were many kinks and bodily aches he would have to work out after being in the pillory for so long. Hobbling down the corridor, he rubbed his neck.

"Not really," he started. "Getting sent to the dungeons gives one a glimmer of hope that they won't *actually* be going to the Tower. Now, if I was sent straight there, *then* I would have panicked. Either that, or being sent to Tyburn." He shivered. "*That* would have had me trembling in the knees."

I shook my head and said nothing.

He got his horse from the stables, and we made our way back to Allington, with Smeaton's violin playing a cheerful tune as we left Whitehall, probably a congratulatory note to Thomas for escaping a potential fate worse than death.

Since it was in the late afternoon, the sun was not as high in the sky, so it didn't bother me much. We got back by nightfall, and I drew Thomas a hot bath to settle his aching body in.

"You know, you don't *act* like a raging, vengeful, demoness of the night," he quipped, as he sat in the water while I rubbed his back.

"Only when provoked," I answered, and playfully yanked on one of his unruly curls. "You took a great risk doing what you did. I was surprised the king was in such a generous mood and spared your life."

"I couldn't see why he would not. After all, they weren't able find any so-called *evidence* to convict me of adultery." He looked up at me and grinned. I exhaled in annoyance.

"As if evidence is needed all the time," I spat. "Look at what happened to *me*! To George! To Smeaton!"

He lowered his gaze again as I ran some clean, warm water over his head. "Have you... decided on what you will do... after you've had your revenge?"

"No," I said plainly. "I will think on that some more when I come to it."

He paused for a while before he spoke again. "Anne--"

"*No*," I quickly answered, dumping more water over his head. This time he coughed and spat out some water. "Why not?"

"I've *told* you why not! Please, Thomas. Life is precious. Don't throw it away on something so frivolous."

"You think your new life is *frivolous*?"

I gave him a look, but he ignored it.

"But Anne, it's like you've been given a second chance!"

"A second chance at *what*? Everything I knew is no more!"

"Then what am I?" he asked angrily.

"You are a server of the Privy Council... *again*... so *act* like it."

He exhaled, sounding despondent, as I left him to finish bathing.

***

Thomas and I did not talk much after our little spat. I often wandered England's green hills, but in the moonlight, her lands looked more like a silvery, dark gray. I had no actual direction to my wanderings; I simply basked in the bit of peace I had in her quiet atmosphere.

I never wandered her hills alone, however. There were always drifting spirits abound -- some women, some men, some soldiers, and every once in a while, a child. Some I could see, some I could only sense their presence. Some would try to speak to me, but I could not hear them. I began to wonder if there were different 'levels' to the land of the dead, and wondered which level *I* was on.

Most of those ghosts were not a pleasant sight either, often taking me by surprise, as they reflected the pains of their death. Some had rope marks around their necks, while some had partial or missing heads. Some had been shot, as a single hole was left in the middle of their foreheads or chest, phantom blood draining from the wounds. They often lingered around their death sites; many trees having been accomplices to their demise. Remnants of rotting bodies hung and swayed from their lowest branches, picked to pieces by ravens or crows.

England's ruler could be very cruel, indeed, and just once, I wished he could have seen the fruits of his injustices that he bestowed on the innocent. Had he no mercy, the inability to show some clemency to the weak?

On the night before his second appearance to the king, Thomas apologized to me, so I accepted. That morning, a carriage was prepared for him, and he and I got in, myself under my usual invisibility guise.

The king reinstated him as a member of the Privy Council once more, and Thomas lavished the king with graces. Thomas was also given his own private chambers at the palace, which he humbly accepted. This was also a nice convenience for me, until he had a mind to start whoring again. It was during those nights that Smeaton kept me company instead.

We talked as we walked the more quieter corridors of Whitehall Palace. He updated me on the health of Anthony, the guard I nearly killed. The physicians had him sectioned off in an area of the palace not frequented by many, to keep a close watch on him. Thinking he had a fever, they bled him, hoping to rid his body of such toxic humors -- and then it was rumored that Anthony scared off the physicians by drinking the blood they expelled from his body.

"Why would he do such a thing, Anne?" he asked me, and I dreaded the worst.

"Perhaps he is becoming like me," I answered. "I pray it is not true."

I began to worry about another as well. As I promenaded around court during dinner hours, I would notice Thomas keeping to himself while the merriment around him was nonstop. He kept a watchful eye on the women of court -- those who were without gentlemen callers, fiancés or husbands. His look was more predatory, sinister, and hungry-like.

Other nights I would notice he would drink excesses of wine, as if he could not slake his thirst. Worse still, he would imbibe to his heart's content, *without* getting drunk. The puckish twinkle in his eyes had long since disappeared. I also noticed Suffolk keeping an eye on him, just as he promised, and right now, that was not a good thing. I needed to find out what was wrong with Thomas before Suffolk did, but there were moments that even Thomas escaped my own watchful eye, gone for hours at a time.

Another night, I happened to catch him hovering over an intoxicated woman at court. He stood behind her chair, his hands massaging her shoulders, putting her at ease. Her head lolled back and she smiled at him in her drunken stupor. Thomas leaned forward and kissed her neck. He lingered there longer than he should have, and I noticed two small rivulets of blood running down the front of her chest. I gasped.

Dear God in heaven, *no*...

Thomas *was* becoming like me! His slow-growing taste for blood was increasing!

Realizing his folly, he covered the woman's neck and quickly led her out of court... and I knew exactly where they were going.

***

By the time I arrived at Thomas's chambers, I could hear the squeals and moans of their carnal pleasures before I even reached the door. I snuck into the room. The woman now on the bed and positioned on her hands and knees, Thomas roughly took her from behind, his pelvis thrusting nonstop as he gripped her hips in heated fervor.

Her animalistic cries were getting louder, and Thomas kept thrusting with such a ferocity I never knew he had. At the height of his orgasm, he roared and leaned forward, fangs extended, biting into the woman's neck.

She cried out, more in surprise than fear, for I was certain she did not understand what was happening, or what Thomas had become.

Unable to hold his weight any longer, the woman collapsed forward on the bed, but Thomas had not let up on his sexual cravings, nor his thirst for blood. Still grinding his pelvis against her buttocks, he moaned between swallows of blood.

It took me a moment to realize the woman had stopped making noises. I rushed over to them, yanking Thomas by the back of his hair. His teeth and lips were covered in blood. I tossed him to the floor, his manhood still erect, bobbing in wanton impatience from the interruption.

"For God's sake, woman! What is the meaning of you disturbing me in the middle of having my fun?" he exclaimed, as he rubbed the back of his head.

"Fool! Your wench is *dead*," I snapped, gripping her up by her hair and shaking her lifeless body about. "You've killed her in your insatiability!"

Thomas blinked, trying to get a handle on the situation as his manhood fell flaccid. "I--I just did that to her? I drank her bl... *her b--?*" Thomas couldn't even say the word as he wiped his mouth, smearing blood on the back of his hand, the look on his face incredulous.

I tilted my head. "You mean, this is the first time you've done this?"

He paused. "There were times when I had this... *urge* for something. I thought it was always my simple self wanting a drink, but the urge grew strongest when I was near a woman." He shook his head. "But I've *never* went as far as I have *just now*!" He got up, throwing on his chemise and breeches, then gripped his hair in frustration. "What am I going to do? I killed this poor woman! What if I get found out?"

"I swear, Thomas," I started, grabbing the dead woman by her hair again and dragging her off the bed with a thump, her limbs askew. "One of these days, your foolish antics will leave you on the rack to rot!" I tried redressing her, but clothing a dead body is no easy task. With bumbling difficulty, we both got her garments on as best we could, and I took her corpse out of the castle, dumping her body in a nearby creek. I told him to stay within the castle, and *purposely* under Suffolk's watchful eye, so he would not be blamed for the 'murder' in case her body was somehow found.

***

I paced the floor of Thomas' chambers as I watched him, sitting on his bed, clutching his sheets. Some of them had smatterings of blood on them.

I sniffed and put a hand on my hip. "At worst, someone could say you bedded a virgin."

He gave a single-tuned, off-key laugh. "Sure. Be blamed for ruining a woman's virtue. As if I need to look any more wrongful in the Duke's eyes." He turned to me, a look of pity on his face. "How do you do it, Anne? How do you... *drink blood* from another person? The idea of it makes me sick, and yet... I *craved* it. I *wanted* it. And I took it all from that woman!"

I sighed, and sat down beside him. "It feels instinctual to me, since drinking blood is necessary in order for me to survive like this. I know how to control my cravings, and stave them off for days at a time. The first time I drank from you, I took just enough to satisfy my needs, as I did the second time. Unfortunately, being under my thumb as well as my donor has caused you to be afflicted as well. You tried putting off your cravings, which is why you went on a blooding frenzy."

Thomas shivered, giving me a look of despair. "If I didn't love you so much, I'd hate you right now."

"Sometimes, I wish you did," I muttered. "That way, you wouldn't be in the predicament you're in now."

Thomas tried to make light of the situation. "Perhaps it's all part of God's grand design! We'll never really know until it's time, right?"

I snorted at him and rolled my eyes. "Really, Thomas, this is *not* part of God's grand design. That's stretching it quite a bit."

He sighed, knowing he would not be able to cheer me up. "So, how will I go about conducting things, now that I'm... well, you know."

"Your feeding should last you a while now. Nevertheless, if you ever get such cravings again, *tend* to them. Do not put them off, or you might get careless and wind up being caught next time. Make sure your victim is one that won't be missed, and make sure you are in a secluded area, far away from prying eyes."

Thomas nodded and gave a rascally smirk. "I guess I really will have to stay indoors *now*, won't I?"

I glared at him. "I ought to *cane* you, Thomas Wyatt."

He embraced me, smiled, and laughed. It was nice that *he* found the humor in all of this... because *I* never would.

Chapter Seven

The days continued onward like any other, and my boredom was increasing. It's true that idle hands make work for the devil, and in my irritation for amusement, I made up yet another cruel game.

Court still was not as mirthful as when I was queen, or, I'll even admit, when Jane was still alive, and the throne that sat to Henry's right was still empty. Whenever they would come to visit court, Mary would sit to Henry's left, as would my Elizabeth, making for a very empty looking and dismal family portrait, but this particular evening, he sat alone.

Henry still dressed in all black garbs, a silent profession of his continued mourning to everyone. Two fingers to his temple, he stared blankly into the crowds, probably as bored as I was.

As I paced around court, figuring out what to do to disrupt things, I heard the thrum of Smeaton's violin before he appeared.

"My Lady!" he said, bowing before me. "Good to see you this evening! How may I be of service to you?"

"Help me liven things up around here," I answered. "This place feels as gloomy as a graveyard. Even so, I bet the dead are more animated than *this* bunch."

"If you'll allow me, my dear Anne, I feel like hitting people tonight. I heard someone make a rather rash comment about my playing earlier! 'That annoying, ghostly, Whitehall violinist', someone said I was!"

I slowly scoured the court for objects to toss, and my eyes rested on a pile of apples.

"I hereby declare this night, *Apple Night*," I said playfully, and Smeaton looked confused.

"Apple Night?"

"*Meaning*... you can go about doing whatever antics you wish... so long as you use *apples* in your trickery."

A huge smile crossed Smeaton's face.

We appeared before the dining table, several people passing us as they went about their business. Whistling, Smeaton casually looked around, spotting someone in particular.

"There he is," he said to himself, then made an apple levitate using sheer force of will. Smeaton hurled it at a pompous, young fop who was talking to a lady. He flinched in surprise and rubbed the back of his head as the lady snickered at him.

"Now I feel better!" Smeaton said. "Silly twat."

I glanced at the king next, and then gave a cunning grin as I leaned against a wall. "I challenge you to a dare, Smeaton."

"I always love a challenge, Anne, you *know* that."

My grin grew wider. "I dare you… to hit the *king*."

Smeaton gasped, mockingly putting a hand to his chest as if surprised by my dare. "Anne! How *could* you think of making me do such a thing?" He put his hand out, making another apple rise, and tossed it across the full length of the room. I don't think anyone saw it fly past them. The next thing we knew, the king's crown was knocked off of Henry's head and fell to the floor with a loud clang.

Those closest to him stopped in the middle of whatever they were doing and gasped. Henry jumped up from his throne, all the blood rushing to his face in anger.

"SIMPLETONS!" he bellowed. "BRAINLESS INGRATES!" He picked up the apple Smeaton tossed. "I'll crush the hand of whoever had the audacity to throw this at me!"

I felt Smeaton's cool, ghostly arms wrap around my shoulders as he buried his face in my neck, trying to prevent himself from laughing. Even I had to cover my mouth. Smeaton had outdone himself this time.

Henry has his groom pick up his crown and check to see if it would need repairing. He took it to the smithy immediately.

Henry demanded everyone stay until someone admitted to his or her folly. Since no one confessed by the time court was over, everyone who attended that evening was banished until someone confessed, Henry ominously reminding them that they were fortunate he did not have every single one of them put in the stocks or the pillory for their foolhardiness.

"Way to go, Smeaton," I said, and chuckled. "I think you have me beat *this* go 'round."

He grinned and folded his arms, raising an eyebrow at me. "You'll have to think of something more challenging next time, Anne. That one was too easy!"

"*Anything* should be easy, when you don't have to worry about being punished for it," I mentioned, picking up one last apple from the bottom of the pile. It was fairly squashed, overripe and nearing rot. Smeaton looked at it.

"What's that for?"

"Oh, nothing really. Just going to pay someone a visit," I answered with a grin. "I'll talk to you soon, Smeaton, and next time, I hope to have a better challenge for you!"

Once again, Thomas was in his chambers, having more 'fun time' with another wench. It was a wonder his privies hadn't fallen off yet.

I entered his chambers, cursing the door when it squeaked. But neither one paid the noise any mind; they were too busy having at it. I thanked the stars they were finishing up; I had no desire to listen to their gleeful moaning as they tussled about.

He and the woman reached orgasm, and they collapsed, side by side. I was also thankful he decided not to bite this particular one.

Since I was invisible, the only thing that was out of place was the apple, 'hovering' in midair.

I made my way to the bed, both of them still panting, recuperating from their ordeal. It took a moment, but the woman stopped and stared at the looming apple before her.

Still staring, she reached over, feeling for Thomas' hand. Once she had it, she gripped it hard.

"Ow, woman! What's the matter with--" Thomas stopped in mid sentence as he finally saw the apple as well, and then groaned, flopping back onto his pillow, as he already knew it was me.

Still, that did not stop my fun.

I slowly waved the apple in front of her, and she began hyperventilating.

"Thomas! Thomas! What is this? Are your chambers haunted by the Whitehall ghosts?"

"My whole *life* is haunted," he grumbled, not even looking at my antics as he covered his face in annoyance. "Quit it, will you?" I heard his muffled voice say to me through his pillow.

I giggled, making the woman whimper in growing fear.

"Thomas... something just *laughed*! Did you not hear it?"

"Yes, I heard it," he answered dryly. "And I wish such impish ghosts would stop *pestering* me!"

Miffed, I hurled the apple at the woman. The fruit was so soft; it actually exploded upon contact with her forehead, foul juices and brown pulp spraying everywhere. She yelped like a scared puppy, and I laughed aloud. *That* sent her screaming out of Thomas' chambers, clothes in hand, stark naked.

"Really Anne, was that *necessary?*" he snapped, pulling the sheets up over himself in a huff.

"Oh, don't be so cross with me, Thomas," I said, reappearing and sitting down on his bed. "I thought that was actually amusing. You should have seen the look on her face when the apple hit her right between her eyes! Besides, at least I waited until you got your jollies."

He folded his arms. "I wouldn't *have* to go through this if you would just let me love *you*, instead. Not being able to have you in my arms like I used to is torture!"

I faced him, surprised at his remark. "I'll never understand you, Thomas. Truth be told, I hold no such desires anymore."

Thomas grabbed me, catching me off guard, and tossed me onto my back. He hovered over me, grinning.

"Is that so?" he insisted, his tongue plunging into my mouth, engaging me in a long, deep kiss.

***

Despite his *very* forward advances, I did not let him have his way with me that night. Perhaps it was the lingering guilt of what I was and what I had done to him, which made me so withdrawn from such pleasures. Still, other creeping matters to attend to were very distracting from my original objective.

The following weeks were plagued with dark mystery. A few women were found around court, days apart, looking pale and sick, some claiming to have been violated by a horrid creature that 'looked like a man, but with the face of a demon'. Thomas already heard of the incidents, and was charged with finding out who the miserable excuse for a man was, and have him put on the rack, and then hanged. Coincidentally, Anthony had disappeared from his private chambers, the physicians having no idea what happened to him.

Henry had called those same physicians and his council members to a meeting, wanting to know why Anthony disappeared, and for them to give him a full report of Anthony's progress while he was in their care, up until his disappearance.

"It seems as though the young gentleman suffered from a sort of mania... a hysteria, if you will," said the first physician. "He also had frequent night sweats, and constantly complained of stomach pains."

"Of course, we need not remind you of our earlier progress reports, when he mentioned a *woman* was to blame for his malady," said the second one.

"And this same woman is said to have attacked him," Henry added stiffly.

"Correct. And then there was the horrifying incident of us bleeding young Anthony to try and stave off his illness, only to witness him moments later, drinking his own blood from the very same pan we used to bleed him."

Henry's eyes widened in disgust, but he said nothing.

"His progress only got worse from there," the first physician continued. "He lost all comprehension of speech, communicating to us in grunts, and growls. His mannerisms became more animal like... and then, he escaped from his room. We haven't seen him since!" There was a look of panic in his eyes as he gripped his hands so tightly, his knuckles began turning white.

"It's obvious he's psychotic," Henry stated, "and I suspect he is the one who violated those women at court." He looked at Thomas. "I put you in charge of finding him and sending him immediately to the Tower. Take all the men you need to hunt him down."

And so, Thomas and his troops spent the next couple of days hunting down Anthony. In that span of time, the women whom Anthony attacked started sweating profusely and complaining of stomach pains as well. Word quickly spread that there was a possibility of the 'sweating sickness' returning, putting people in a panic.

Thomas fared no better from this situation, either. Now forced to go outdoors and search the grounds, he began to pale and sweat, eventually passing out. He was taken back to his chambers and waited on by the physicians. Unfortunately, during Thomas' incapacity, three more women were found -- violated, sick, and feverish.

I had to put a stop to Anthony's evildoings, and quickly.

Another rumor began to spread as well. One that was more sinister and archaic. As I roamed the London slums, I found out that the women of the court were not the only victims to this strange, perverted abuse. Here in the poorer parts of the town, women were being violated by some strange, 'naked man with the devil's eyes'. They believed the man to be some sort of incubus, a creature of the night that sexually preyed on hapless women, especially in their sleep. I used to believe such things were nothing more than the twisted fantasies of depraved women, but with myself being a creature of darkness now, I had to consider the possibility of such a creature being real.

I knew Anthony was no such thing, but his sexual appetites I did find very peculiar.

I continued investigating the towns around Whitehall, not interacting with anyone, only listening to possible clues as to Anthony's whereabouts. One night, I finally got lucky, as I listened to the panicky talk of a prostitute, exclaiming that a naked man snatched her partner into an alleyway. Once I heard the exact location, I made my way there.

Stopping at the alley entrance, I stared ahead of me.

Anthony's body was streaked with filth and caked mud, but there was no denying that his skin was pale, matching my own complexion. The prostitute was pressed to the dank, cold wall, her legs raised in such a manner that she could not escape, as Anthony plunged his manhood deep into her several times. His face was hidden in the large curls of her hair, no doubt draining her of her blood, as he continually thrust himself into the dying woman, grunting in carnal delight. Not one sound came from the woman. I knew she was done for.

Anthony still took no notice of me, which was good. I snuck up behind him, and then, he sensed me. He turned, and even his eyes matched mine in color, as bright a red as the blood that was smeared across his lips and fangs. He hissed at me, eyes round and nearly glowing. Dropping his nightly meal, he pushed me over, running away from me.

"Damn it," I cursed to myself, getting up and running after him. Anthony was beyond all sense and reason. He was a wild *thing* -- and he had to *die*.

I tried to follow him, but he had long gone. He disappeared like a thief in the night.

Annoyed at my lack of success in catching Anthony, I headed back to Thomas' chambers.

***

"Anne, that was foolish of you, going about the town at night, looking for that... *monster*," Thomas, spat, slowly sitting up in bed.

"How are you feeling?" I asked him.

"Better. I'm surprised I didn't go up in smoke, considering what happened to you the first time," he said with a half smirk.

"Perhaps this curse is different for everyone," I mentioned. "Anthony is completely feral, like some untamed animal. I wonder how he got to be that way," I said to myself, staring out of his window.

"My bets are on him drinking his own blood being the reason for his insanity," Thomas quipped. "After all, we drink *others'* blood, not *our own*. Surely that might have done *some* damage to his brain."

My eyes lit up. "You make a very valid point, Thomas, but how he got to be that way isn't the real problem. We have to catch him and kill him before he attacks more women."

"The Duke of Suffolk is leading the troops into capturing him now, but I can relay that Anthony was spotted in the town."

I nodded at Thomas. "Do you need anything before I go?"

"Go? Why not stay with me and keep me company?"

I paused. "Because you'll only try to bed me again, Thomas. You *should* focus on recuperating, so you can help everyone catch that creature."

He gave me a malicious grin. "You know, in a way, he's like your son, and your responsibility. After all, *you* created him... just like how you created *me*."

"You are *nothing* like him, Thomas," I snapped. "And don't you *ever* mention that to me again!"

I slammed his chamber door before I had a mind to throw him across the room for his insolence.

***

I stormed down the corridor, almost too angry to think. How dare Thomas make such a comment?

But in some strange, perverse way, Anthony *was* my responsibility.

I carelessly left him for dead, and he *survived*, now crazed with primal instincts and a primitive mind, plus a horrible lust for blood, because no one was able to guide him in his new un-life.

Every single one of the ladies' conditions were worsening, and I was completely powerless to stop it. Anthony had attacked seven women in total, and it was seven women too many. What if they wound up exactly like me, or worse, had a mind like *him*? This curse, I now realized, acted like a communicable disease, and would spread like wildfire if Anthony wasn't captured and the women treated -- *if* there even was such a thing as a 'cure' for what I had. And it was all my fault!

Whitehall was practically deserted after the rumors of sweating sickness prevailed, although the physicians were undoubtedly sure that the sickness was *not* the case this time. On closer observance, the physicians also noticed two small puncture wounds on the victim's necks -- the same wounds they noticed on Anthony. With this new discovery, they immediately reported it to the king, who rubbed his chin in deep thought, just as baffled as they were.

"Not only do we have to capture Anthony, but we must find the one who started it all. We have to go back to the beginning. We need to find this mysterious *woman*."

I smirked and shook my head. I found it astonishing that it was taking them so long to piece all the little details together.

Once Thomas was well again, he continued the search for Anthony, while Henry now charged Suffolk in hunting down 'the woman'. I chuckled to myself. This would give me a chance to play with the Duke for a while... at least until I got tired of him.

***

Daffodils here, a little warning there -- my tricks were driving Suffolk mad with frustration. The funniest joke I pulled on the Duke was leading him down a hall with a single line of my favorite flowers. They led up to a portrait of Henry that I had placed on the floor and turned upside down, immersing it in a pile of rotted food scraps until Henry's head was covered. Above the painting, I had scrawled on the wall in blood:

Henry or Suffolk... who is the bigger fool?

The Duke was not too happy with *that* discovery. I don't even think he mentioned that one to Henry!

Court had nearly dissolved, and I could tell Henry was slipping more and more into depression and frequent mood swings. He spent a lot of time alone again, not much in mourning, but more worried about the continued riots concerning the religious reformation, and the 'nonsensical happenings' around the palace.

Smeaton joined me again, and I told him of the recent events. He told me that he saw Anthony running naked across a cemetery late one night, howling as if he were one with the wolves. I immediately alerted Thomas about it, and he and his men went out on another hunt. To my joy and surprise, they finally caught him, but not without Anthony putting up a good fight. Since the king wanted him brought back alive, the troops had to execute some creative tactics to capture Anthony without killing him outright. All I know was that it involved using *a lot* of rope, as Anthony broke free of their bonds not once, but *twice*. He was also shot in both his legs to prevent him from running.

They dragged Anthony behind a horse as they made their way back to the palace. That alone should have been more than enough to kill him, despite the king's orders, but to their horror, Anthony remained *alive*, disfigured to the point where half of his face had been scraped clean away, exposing shredded muscle and bone. His shoulders, buttocks and legs suffered the same fate -- and through it all, Anthony's tenacity in trying to escape was relentless. He gnashed his teeth and lunged at Thomas and his troops like a maniac; a crazed *beast*. Once they were at the palace, they used a staff, and attached Anthony's bindings to it, continuing to drag him to the dungeons.

Once he was there and securely locked away, Thomas reported to the king of their good news in capturing Anthony, and Henry rejoiced, telling him he would inform them of what punishment Anthony would be given before he was tried. Thomas took careful consideration in telling the king that Anthony was not 'normal', and should not be tried like a regular person. Henry was not sure what he meant by that until Thomas encouraged Henry to see Anthony for himself. Once he did, Thomas mentioned to me that the look in Henry's eyes was unfathomable, as if he couldn't comprehend how Anthony could have survived such mangling and fatal bodily wounds, while still showing such ferocity, especially when he bared two large, white fangs at Henry in sheer rage.

To put some sort of logic to the situation, however unrealistic it may have sounded to Henry, he declared Anthony as being possessed by a demon, no longer being of sound mind, with no hope of redemption or ever returning to a normal life. He sentenced him to a day on the rack before he was to be burned at the stake.

The guards feared going near Anthony, afraid of becoming just like him if he bit or merely touched him. Thomas and Suffolk managed to strap him to the rack, stretching Anthony until they nearly pulled all his limbs out of their sockets, and still, Anthony gave no sign of letting up, growling, hissing and snapping at them the more they tortured him.

Then finally, the breaking moment. Anthony's shoulders were finally pulled out of whack, as were his hip joints, and he howled and wailed in agony. One leg that had already been badly damaged by his horse-dragging, had been pulled apart altogether. His screams were so loud, you could hear just the faintest echo of them in the nearby corridors adjacent to the dungeons.

That night, Thomas could barely take his clothes off. I drew him another hot bath, and he settled his aching body within the water.

"You don't have to keep doing this for me," he said, wincing as he sat down. "Although I greatly appreciate it."

"This was a very long night for you," I started, rubbing his back with a sponge. "Who would have imagined that Anthony would become the creature that he is." I looked down. "It's so *frightening*."

"Be of good cheer, Anne! The beast is caught, and all can stop fearing him."

"And yet, I hope his fate does not befall those ill women as well," I said ominously. "Have the physicians given any word on their condition?"

"The women have been bled, and although they did not partake of their own blood, at least one of them has been found walking the corridors as if in a daze."

"I do not like the sound of that." I gave a long pause. "Perhaps I should kill them."

"Anne!" Thomas looked at me in horror. "At least give them a fighting chance!"

"A fighting chance at what? Recovery from their bane? *My* bane? Nothing the physicians can do will fix their malady! For their malady is *mine*, and there is no cure for it."

"But we don't know that for sure, yet."

"I feel it deep down in my heart, Thomas. There *isn't*."

We were silent for a while as I massaged his shoulders.

"Are you hungry, Thomas? I could go to the kitchens and fetch something for you there."

"I'm more tired than hungry, but I know if I do not eat, I'll surely be hungry later."

"It's not a problem, Thomas, really."

"What if someone sees you?"

I stood up, smiling. "I think I've perfected the act of invisibility quite well now. If anything, they'll sum up any phantom floating food they happen to see as another Whitehall mystery."

"By eyes you go unseen, but physically you're still touchable?"

I nodded. "If someone *were* to bump into me, yes, they would surely feel me. I'll be back soon," I said, closing his chamber door behind me.

As I made my way to the kitchens, I could hear Smeaton's violin, sounding as vibrant and jolly as ever. The halls were very desolate, but I was beginning to prefer them that way.

After stacking a variety of bread, meat, fruit, and cheese into a small cloth, I made my way back to Thomas's quarters.

I had always been so extremely careful up until that point not to be noticed, but my carelessness in allowing the bundle of food to be so plainly noticed got me in trouble for the first time in over a year.

Holding the bundle in front of me, I walked down the corridors, not realizing that I was being followed until it was too late. The next thing I knew, a short wooden staff had pierced my body.

I dropped my provisions and screamed in pain, clutching the staff in my hands.

My predator had been Charles, whom I was sure was aiming for the bundle of food. What he did not expect was to hear the scream.

Two other guards flanked the Duke, but all of their expressions showed fear and trepidation. To them, the staff must have looked like it was suspended in mid air, when *technically*, it was suspended through *me*.

I yanked it out of my midsection, nothing but red coating my hands and the weapon. I hurled it back at them, although I aimed for no one in particular. They yelled in shock as they saw 'phantom blood' all over it.

While they were still busy with figuring out how that was possible, I grabbed the rations and fled as quickly as I could back to Thomas' quarters.

Lying on his bed, Thomas jumped when he saw me a bloody mess.

"Dear God! Anne! What happened?" He leapt off the bed and helped me to a chair.

I dropped the bundle beside me when I sat. Thomas shook his head in surprise.

"Anne, I can't *believe* you still brought this back. You should have just ran for your life."

I gave a weak smile. "You were hungry, were you not?"

"You staying alive is more important than bringing me food!"

I gestured to the bed, so he picked me up and carried me to it, gently placing me down on the sheets.

"It was Suffolk," I said between grunts. "He spotted me... somewhat."

"You mean he spotted what you were carrying."

I nodded my reply.

Thomas put his hand on top of my wound, his eyes getting watery. "Don't die Anne. Please. Not now..."

"My time isn't up yet," I said. "But he *will* get his due, and *soon*."

***

The day of Anthony's execution was a grisly one. I had finally healed up enough to boldly attend his execution among the rest of the crowd.

Anthony had to be pulled by cart to his destination. He was taken from the Tower to Tyburn and tied to the stake. Most of his energy had been spent while being tortured, and the crowds were aghast at his appearance. He was quite literally a dead man walking, something out of one's worst nightmare. With half a face left, a missing eye, and the rest of his body in shredded, distorted pieces, the crowds mumbled that he was surely a creation of the Devil to have lived so long in such a state.

The sun was beaming down that morning. Thank heavens for the cloak Thomas had given me.

Anthony still moaned and growled, writhing under the ropes that kept him fastened to the stake, and hungrily snapped at the executioner as all of his charges were read off. Anthony was convicted of all the 'pranks' that had happened throughout the castle, being adulterous, and committing treason against the king.

Anthony's writhing was growing more irritated as he squinted at the sun and moaned in agony. To everyone's shock, he suddenly burst into flames, fire and black smoke emanating from his body and trailing in the wind. Talk amongst the crowd was frenzied and loud as the executioner stood there gawping, with a torch in his hand. Not knowing what else to do, he touched it to the straw, setting it afire. But, the unexplained had already been seen and witnessed by all. Anthony had been burning *before* the executioner's torch even touched him.

***

Word of Anthony's 'curious death' had made its way back to the king. He did not say much on the account; he was merely glad that the 'evil, crazed lunatic' was dead. To Henry, it was one less problem to worry about.

His *new* problems were just about to start.

Charles was making his rounds about the palace one evening, when I snuck up behind him, jumped on his back, and grabbed his hair, yanking his head back to expose his throat.

"Pompous bastard," I hissed in his ear, then mercilessly slit his throat.

Suffolk gurgled and clutched at his wound, collapsing to his knees, a dark red waterfall flowing freely between his fingers. Wide eyed, he looked around in a panic, noticing no one was around him. I think that knowledge scared him more than his pending death. I laughed in triumph.

Three guards rounded a corner and spotted the Duke on the floor, and the ever-growing pool of blood under him. They ran towards Charles, one of them tearing at their own sleeve, wrapping it around the Duke's neck to stanch the flow. In minutes, the cloth was soaked through and bright red. They picked him up and cried out for more help, carrying him away to the physicians.

Damn them to hell!

A few days later, and to my great annoyance, the physicians

managed to keep him alive, but barely. He was saved by their rather barbaric and unskilled suturing abilities, literally fastening his skin together with a needle and catgut. Suffolk had lost a great deal of blood, and he was still not in the clear. Infection could still set in; as it most likely would with wounds so large, so Henry had many of his own servants tend to Charles day and night, caring for Suffolk's wounds by using fresh poultices and bandages.

It took a couple of weeks, but the Duke became stronger, strong enough to mention that his attacker was unseen, but heard, and as quick as the Devil.

I never told Thomas that it was I who slit Suffolk's throat, but he did not have to ask. He already knew.

"I never believed you'd have such a wicked heart," he said to me one evening. His look was of genuine surprise, with a hint of sadness.

"You speak of wickedness, when it was *he* who lanced *me* with a staff?" I said with incredulity as I put my hands on my hips.

Thomas frowned and sighed. "Touché."

"Besides, if I did to him what he did to me, then he *would* have died."

"Like a slit throat *wouldn't* do the trick?"

"At least I didn't cut him *all* the way across his neck."

"The Duke is the king's *best* friend! If he had lost *him* on top of Jane's death..." Thomas shook his head. "He looks near ready to pull his hair out."

"The fun's just starting, dear Thomas," I said with a wry smile. "For his dear Jane isn't quite out of the picture just yet."

***

With Suffolk now out of my hair, I could concentrate on getting my revenge with Henry, and I wanted it to be *good*.

Merriment at court was still at a minimum, but at least more people had returned upon Anthony's death. The culprit now caught and destroyed, it seemed as if everyone could rest easy again.

Two of Anthony's victims had died, but no public announcement was made. They were quietly buried in St. Peter's churchyard. It seems as if they had been forgotten about, amidst all the commotion of Anthony's own death.

Henry sat in the king's chair, looking extremely perturbed as he watched the crowd. I was sure Suffolk was still on his mind.

I grabbed a handful of grapes from a table, nibbling at them slowly. They did not have much of a taste to me, and I was saddened. I so loved grapes when I was alive. The only thing that would satisfy me now was one's life essence.

I did not get a chance to dwell on that long, as Smeaton appeared before me.

"I heard Anthony's execution was brutal," he said. "Is it true he burned himself by some mysterious force?"

"Creatures of the dark cannot tolerate daylight," I answered. "Even I can't, which is why I wear a cloak so often. The sun itself was the cause for his burning. I can catch on fire as well, as I did the first time I returned to this world. I burned my hand in the first rays of morning's light."

Smeaton shuddered. "At least I don't have to worry about such things. When the sun comes up, I sort of... *drift off* into some other place, almost like taking a nap, until nightfall, of course." He gazed around the court, and sniffed. "Poor Majesty. He looks as if he's lost his best friend."

"He almost *did*," I spat. Smeaton looked at me and blinked.

"*You*? You're the one who almost killed the Duke of Suffolk?" He shook his head in disbelief. "My God, woman! When I heard about someone slitting Charles' throat, I assumed it was an enemy of the king, or a foe of Charles'!"

"A die for a die, Smeaton. He nearly killed *me*."

"He--? But *how*?"

"A wooden staff to my midsection nearly did the trick. It took me a couple of days to recuperate from *that* ordeal."

"Oh, my dear, sweet Anne!" He attempted to hug me, but all I felt was a cold, light pressure around me.

"There now, Smeaton. The worst is over -- but not for the king."

He glanced over at Henry, who looked like he was deep in thought. "What are we doing to him tonight?"

"A bit of a tease," I answered, and then whispered my plan to him.

We approached Henry without any difficulties. When I picked up a chair and carefully placed it beside him, it took him a moment to realize the difference; he had been so preoccupied with whatever was on his mind.

He stared at the chair, wide-eyed in disbelief.

I had purposely set the chair on his right side, and eased myself into it, trying my best not to make too much noise.

Smeaton was behind me, and on my cue, placed his ghostly hand on top of the king's.

It took few seconds, but Henry finally sensed something was touching him. He slowly peered down at his hand, Smeaton covering his mouth to prevent himself from laughing in the king's ear.

I focused hard, trying to remember the sound of Jane's voice before I leaned towards His Majesty.

"Henry, my love," I whispered to him. "Henry, oh how I miss you."

Henry's eyes widened in distress, disbelieving at first, then, he burst into tears. He covered his face and sobbed, quickly jumping up and rushing out of court.

Smeaton finally gave himself permission to laugh, and I gave a subtle grin.

He would never be over Jane, *never*. As long as I continued to torture him, I would not *allow* him to be, especially since he loved his *precious* Jane *so* much.

***

I told Thomas of Smeaton's and my latest handiwork, and he actually looked upset.

"You're gong to drive him truly mad you know," Thomas said to me. "The king has always seemed unstable, but the things you're doing to him now… if he *does* go mad, who would be king? Prince Edward is still an infant, and God forbid Jane's brother would, ipso facto, become king. He's not too well liked by the council."

"He always seems to have a cold disposition, but no matter. I will not drive the king *that* far. He's very rational minded… when he's not angered." I gave an evasive smirk.

"And do you seriously believe he's in a 'rational' state at this time, Anne? The man has lost a wife and gained a son in the process, and is terrified of his child dying from some obscure illness every day. Riots still break out on occasion, and with all the morbid, cruel, grotesque things you've been doing around the castle…" Thomas shook his head. "I would not want to be in the king's shoes, not for all the money in the world. Especially if *you* were haunting me."

I chuckled to myself. "I'll take that as a *compliment*, Thomas."

***

A few days later, I started getting a strange, nagging feeling in the pit of my stomach. Something seemed to be calling me home. I had no idea why, as my business with my father had been finished.

Nevertheless, I took leave of Whitehall and made my way to Hever once more as soon as the sun faded from view.

The castle was bleak and colder than normal, and all the mirrors were draped in black cloth.

"Hello?" I called out, and then thought it silly of me to do. I investigated several rooms, finding no one. What *drew* me here? It was not like I could willingly recall fond memories of this place anymore.

I wandered outside, and a carriage was pulling up. It was Mary and her husband, William. He helped her out of the carriage, and they made their way into the castle. Baffled, I followed them back in.

Mary was sniffing, a few tears rolling down her cheek. She walked over to one of the mirrors I saw, and pulled the cloth from it.

She looked at her reflection in the mirror as she spoke to William. "Poor father. It came so unexpected…"

"It amazes me, how strong you can be, Mary. Your father rejected you, rejected our *marriage*, stripped you of your allowance, and nearly left you penniless! And yet, you can still show love for the man who treated you so unkindly."

She turned to face him. "True, he may have been unkind and often cruel, but he was still my father, and the only father I'll ever have. That in itself means something to me. Now he is gone. My whole family is gone." She began to weep, and William held her in his arms until she was able to compose herself.

A sudden coldness seemed to trickle through ever single vein in my body.

Our father was dead.

If Mary had been alone, I would have shown myself to her, but William was there. I had to get her attention somehow.

"Hever will soon be completely dissolved, and become property of

The Crown. It's best we take what little possessions we can salvage, before it's too late."

They went upstairs, which gave me a moment to think. I sat in a chair, still in shock.

Mary was brave indeed, and sometimes, a lot stronger in heart than I was. She could be so forgiving, so easy of virtue. These were the qualities that she always retained, that even *I* knew I could not always possess, no matter how hard I tried.

Our father had died, and she could feel remorse for the loss.

I could not.

When Mary and William came back downstairs with a few small items, I tried getting her attention by waving a tapestry on the wall. William had already exited the castle, and the tapestry caught her eye. She took a step back, unsure of what to think.

"Mary," I whispered, then made myself appear before her.

Her eyes widened, then she calmed down when she realized it was me.

"Good heavens, sister, you put me in a fright! I thought I'd never see you again!" We embraced. "How did you know?"

I looked down. "I--I had a strange feeling something was amiss."

She gave a knowing grin. "Despite whatever malice you held for him, family always has a connection with each other."

Those were unnerving words, and I did not know what to say. Mary truly had a sort of peace within her soul that I was never able to grasp.

"Where is he buried?"

"At Hever Church," she answered. "If you want, we can go there."

"What about William?"

"We'll both sit on one side of the carriage. You can sit across from us, next to the family possessions."

"Very well," I said, making myself invisible as we approached the carriage together. For some odd reason, we both began to smile. It was as if we were playing a game by keeping my presence a secret from William. And for that moment, I managed to capture a bit of my childhood spirit.

She mentioned to William that she wanted to make a final stop at the church, and we got there in no time. William was completely oblivious, as Mary occasionally made quick gestures and smiles at me, despite her not being able to see exactly where I was sitting.

She told William she would be a moment, and walked with me to our father's burial site.

He had a modest grave marker, his headstone stating his titles and positions he had during his lifetime, as well as being noted as father of the Queen of England.

We stood there in silence for a moment, as I listened to her quiet sniffs. My eyes rested on the last epitaph of him being father to the queen, and I felt bile rising in my throat.

Mary placed a few flowers at his headstone. "Rest in peace father," she whispered, and then slowly turned to walk away.

When I was sure she would not look back, I spat on his grave.

Chapter Eight

It was as if the visit to my father's final resting place replenished my ambition and determination to see my goals through once more. I would show my enemies no mercy, and I had one more enemy to go. Even so, that final enemy was weakening with every move I made, every torture I bestowed on his callous, ostentatious self.

One more victim of Anthony's rampage had died, leaving four more still surviving. They buried the woman near where she lived. Again, no announcements were made.

More rebels against the religious reformation attacked near Whitehall, and Henry's imperial guards fought back. I found the insurgents' blatant heroism just as honorable as it was foolish -- you cannot strike bullets with swords, and they were far faster than a mere blade.

Everyone felt like they had the need to fight for something, even when it might cost them their very lives. Honor, freedom, faith, devotion... these were some of the things they died for. But, when all those values were lost forever, what would they fight for, then?

Vengeance begets nothing but a vicious cycle of further vengeance. As long as a positive and a negative force collided, there would always be cause for war. I wondered if I should have been heeding my own thoughts, as I watched their frenzied fighting from a high window in the palace.

Getting bored of the men, their guns and their swordplay, I took a walk amongst the gardens that night. Since everyone's focus was on stopping the fighting, the rest of the grounds were empty for the time being.

I sat on a stone bench and gazed into the waters of the lily pad pond. I did not want to focus on anything else, save the moon's reflection on the water. Once more, I sent a silent plea to God to save me from the wretched life he damned me with, and to forgive me of my transgressions. I had done a horrible thing, renouncing my faith, and the punishment was wearing thin.

Ah-ha! There it went again, my vast changes in mood! This nearly drove me as mad as I was making Henry! I just wanted it all to *go away*.

Frustrated, I was about to get up, until I felt a point sticking me in my back.

"Stay down. State your name, and your business here."

I lowered my head and sniffed. Was I getting more careless in my actions lately? I should have kept myself invisible, regardless of it being night. As useful as it was in avoiding contact with people, performing such a trick was always a bit draining on me. Just once, it would have been nice *not* to need it, but...

"I have no name, and my business here is none of yours," I answered in a cold tone.

"Up with you! We will see how quick you are to use your tongue when I take you to the *king*! If you're lucky, you'll only need to beg for forgiveness, and mercy."

"I won't be requiring it... but *you* will."

I pulled my hood down and whipped around, hissing, baring my fangs, my eyes bright in all their red, hellish glory. I startled the guard and he dropped his sword, giving me the opportune moment to strike. I lurched forward, grabbed him, and bit into his neck, tearing at his flesh. Blood poured from his wound as he dropped like a rag doll. I continued feeding from him until he was dry, and then snapped his neck for added measure. I did not need another mishap like Anthony roaming around again.

I looked at the sword at his feet and paused. Grabbing it, I raised it over my head, and swung downward.

I severed the guard's head with a single, clean cut, and then tossed both body parts into the pond. After that menial task, I made my way back into the castle.

Damn these *annoying* humans!

That certainly ruined my quiet time.

***

During the following night, another hellish incident occurred that sent inhabitants of the palace screaming through its halls in terror -- but *I* was not the cause of their screams this time. What? Something was awry, and not *my* fault for a change? I had to investigate.

The screams mostly came from women of the court. As I listened to their hysterical voices, they spoke of a 'ghastly thing that barely resembled a woman', and I shivered. It had to have been one of Anthony's victims. Damn it. I should have gone to *all* their graves and burned them!

Thomas wanted to come with me one night of my search, so I allowed him. Even though I felt that I could search the grounds much faster alone, I did not mind his company that night.

"Do you know where they buried the bodies of those women Anthony killed?" I asked him as we made our way on horseback through the moonlit lands, away from Whitehall.

He nodded, and I followed him to the cemetery. One of the women was buried near her home, which happened to be in Rochford. I hoped this particular dead woman was not the one that happened to be terrorizing everyone. I wanted my sister, her family, and Elizabeth to be safe.

We traveled there first, just in case, but the grave was still untouched. In any case, I didn't want her rising.

I hopped down off my horse, and began to unearth her with my bare hands. Thomas was sullen as he waited for me to finish.

Once I had her uncovered, she barely gave a stench, despite her being in the ground for quite a few days. There was no doubt she would rise unless I did something.

I covered her with straw that was stuffed inside of a bundle that I had attached to my horse. I set the straw on fire next, and then patiently waited.

It took a moment, but suddenly, she sat up and started screaming. Her entire body was aflame as she tried getting out of her grave, writhing and reaching for us.

"Thomas, your sword!" I snapped. He only stared at the flaming body as if in a daze. I snatched his sword from out of the sheath by his waist, and swung.

The dead woman's flaming head went rolling quite a distance from her body… and Thomas *laughed*. I did not find this remotely funny at all, and scoffed at him.

"Have you gone daft? You would have let her escape! Imagine the hysteria of the townspeople seeing her running around, completely on fire!"

Thomas sniffed. "So is this what we have become, Anne? Bounty hunters of the dead, and dead ourselves? Sounds like quite a paradox, don't you think?" He gave another wicked sounding laugh.

I growled at Thomas. "I don't have time for your overemotional mood shifts!" Really! If he started acting like this now, we would never get anything accomplished.

I tossed dirt on the woman's head to put out the flames, and then picked up the charred, smoking, blackened remains. Hard, crusted flesh clung onto her burnt, blackened skull, her two pearly fangs protruding downward in animalistic profession, and in stark contrast to everything else. I grimaced at it before taking it over to her grave and dropping it in without a second thought, the skull falling somewhere near one of her shoulders. The rest of her remains were just as scorched as her skull. We piled the dirt back into her grave, and pushed onward on our little search.

We came back to the chapel after hours of no luck, and decided to finish off the two remaining buried bodies -- but we received quite a shock as we came upon their graves.

Each one had been disturbed, and they both were gone.

I looked around in a panic. The cemetery was silent and still. There were not even the usual nighttime sounds I so enjoyed. I cursed to myself.

"*Now* what am I to do? They're *gone!*" I looked to Thomas. "What if I can't find them in time? What if they create more of our kind?"

"We multiply quickly, just like the vermin we are," he retorted, folding his arms.

"Come off it, Thomas. It is not as if I *asked* for this life. I've *always* upheld my spiritual beliefs and faith! Who would think that out of my anger against it, *this* would happen to me?!"

Thomas stared at me for a moment, opened his mouth as if he were about to say something, then changed his mind.

I was sorry I asked him to come along with me. He really was not much company after all. I would have done much better with Smeaton!

The next nights were plagued with more rumors of evil creatures running about town, trying to maim people and drink the blood of the living. The remaining four women in the physicians' care were going insane, tearing at their clothes, and nearly running around naked. Henry's head physician suggested the women be locked away immediately, for their own safety, but not in bedlam. Whatever they had was unlike the usual maladies of humankind. Henry then suggested leaving them locked up in the dungeons, so that's where the physicians -- as well as with the help of Henry's guards -- put them.

I heard through Smeaton that the dungeon master would try poking them with rods through the small window in their door. It was done out of sheer cruelty, just to see them behave like animals. When they were left alone, they were calm. Angered at how men could be so mindlessly spiteful, I took a trip to the dungeons to have a little 'talk' with the dungeon master, before I had a mind to kill the women myself and put them out of their misery.

As I arrived at their door, what I saw next would have put a brothel to shame.

The dungeon master was sprawled out on the floor, as one of the women had herself impaled upon his manhood, naked, riding him as if he were a wild stallion. Parts of his clothes had been torn away from his body, while another woman sat upon his face as she moaned, her eyes closed and into the moment, as she fondled her own breasts. The other two seemed to be watching them in the utmost patience, crouching near the promiscuous duo, waiting in a very predatory-like stance. The remaining two women were also naked.

The first one rode him harder and faster, trying to force him to climax. His filthy hands groped at her breasts, squeezing them as the two of them bounced together in rhythmic pleasure. When he reached the point of orgasm, he cried out in utter bliss. She only gave him a brief moment to enjoy the aftermath, as the second one jumped off of his face so the first could lunge forward and tear into his neck.

Now he was crying out in agony. The two that were crouching also pounced on him, each attacking a thigh, and the one that was enjoying cunnilingus fed from the inside of his elbow.

He was completely pinned down with no way of escape. In seconds, he would be dead.

I sniffed and grinned, deciding the let them have their little payback.

"What I wouldn't give to be him right now," Smeaton said from behind me. I gasped and turned around.

"You *can't* be serious."

"Well, *before* they started feeding, of course." He grinned at me.

I shook my head. "You *would*, Smeaton."

"I can't deny missing life at court," he continued. "The decadence and debauchery were always quite enjoyable."

In those few moments I engaged in conversation with Smeaton, the dungeon master's blood must have strengthened them. It appeared that first time feedings seemed to have an enormous effect on their physical prowess. We heard a dull sounding *boom* as they destroyed the single prison window they had. I looked through their door again and watched as they leapt through the new exit they made, escaping into the night.

"This is horrible!" I told him, eyes wide, and then spoke softer, making an ominous, prophetic statement. "These creatures will roam England's hills, torturing her people forevermore."

"I'll alert Thomas," Smeaton said, disappearing in front of me.

A short while later, I watched from an empty room as Thomas and five guards rode their horses into the night, hunting down the now *six* undead. I did not worry much for Thomas, as he was one of us, but I hoped the guards would not fall to their predatory antics. Before the night was through, they managed to capture two. Not enough. *All* would have been better, but we dark creatures were crafty things.

I caught Henry in his study, doing the same thing I had been. He leaned against a wall, gazing out of a window as the moon put a faint glow in his immediate area.

"What has become of my kingdom? Why are these vile things happening? What have I done to deserve this?" he said to the moon, or perhaps to God.

I stood a short distance from him and spoke. "The time has come, Henry. The dead are rising from their graves… and it's all thanks to *you*."

He turned and looked at me. My hood was over my head, my face remaining concealed

"Stop right there, woman, and show yourself." He brandished a small knife. "How dare you come here and try to turn my kingdom upside down with your madness! What is this nonsense talk of the dead rising from their graves?"

I remained silent, which, naturally, angered him.

"Speak woman, or by God, I'll *make you* speak!" He waved the knife at me, slowly approaching me.

"That which is dead is not supposed to speak, is it not?" I

answered, giving a cruel laugh before I dashed out of the room.

Henry tried to follow, but I was gone before he reached the door. He gave another cry of anguish that echoed through the corridors of Whitehall.

The following morning, the two captured women were burned at Tyburn. Though they did not catch on fire like Anthony had, they kept screaming and screaming -- much longer than an average person would. They bared their fangs at the dumbfounded crowd until one of them broke free of their restraints and almost fell into the spectators, her charred body running amok until she finally collapsed on her own accord.

Shortly, England was no longer referred to the usual jeering monikers. Such darker events preceded those of before. England was now coined as *The Devil's Haven*. Stories of ghosts, witches and demons were running so rampant, merchants were fearful of doing trade or other business with Henry, which began stressing him out even more. He actually fell sick for nearly a week, only having his physician check in on him, while the Privy Council again tried picking up where Henry had quickly faltered, easing the minds of the townsfolk, the merchants, and anyone else that had questions about England's dire predicament. The Duke was still able to get around with minimal problems, but was unable to talk. He would visit Henry from time to time, to keep him company for a while.

Having nowhere to sit except the king's chair, I sat down, staring at an empty court again, leaning against one arm of the chair, thinking up my next trick for Henry. Footsteps approached moments later, but, knowing it was Thomas, I did not bother with the need to hide. He almost passed through the entire room without noticing me, unless he was ignoring me on purpose. Then, he abruptly stopped, turned to face me, and scowled.

"Sometimes, I wish I had never laid eyes on you."

I sniffed, barely amused. "What brought this thought on *again*?"

"Your devilry… your witchery… the hell you've cast England in!"

I waved him off. "Spare me your righteous outrage, Thomas. You can tell me no more than what I already know. Aren't you tired of talking about it?"

"If only I hadn't fallen in love with you--"

"So you try to blame *me* for your poor, misguided heart? Please,

Wyatt. You dwell too much in the past… *as usual.*"

"As do *you!*" He snickered, a maniacal glint in his eye. "Perhaps I should kill you in your sleep. Maybe *that* will put England out of its misery… *and yours.*"

Enraged, I stood up. "Watch your tongue, Thomas, or you'll quickly find it *missing.*"

Again, he still ignored me as he approached me, slowly drawing his sword. I gave him such a disbelieving look as I watched on. If he truly attempted to kill me, he would be dead before he hit the floor.

"Maybe if I cut off your head? Perhaps *burn* you? Or tie you up and put you out in the fields and wait for the sun to rise?" Tears were welling up in his eyes. "My heart aches to be with you, Anne, and yet *loathes* you just the same!" He took a deep breath before he continued. "You have *no idea* how that felt, Anne! Seeing you in the king's arms, knowing that should have been *me!* And you practically rubbed it in my face every time I saw you! How it hurt my heart that he would love you *over* and *over*... and I, a mere member of his fucking *Privy Council*! All I could do was watch you from afar!"

One thing was for certain, Thomas definitely had a flair for the dramatic. "Then why don't you just go ahead and kill me, then? Free me, and you'll free *yourself* as well."

His shoulders drooped slightly. "No matter what I do, I'll *never* be free of you. The memories will always remain."

"The trick is to not allow the memories consume you! You must have the courage to *move on.*"

He stepped closer, lowering his sword, his cheeks wet with tears. "Perhaps I don't have the courage, Anne. Perhaps I don't *want* it."

"Then you are your own jailer, Thomas, and *no one* will be able to save you."

"*Love* is my jailer. Always has been." We were now face-to-face, and I pushed him away.

"And *that* is your definition of love? How *sad*. Perhaps what is driving you mad is the need for a simple, good fuck. If that's the case, go find yourself a silly wench to sate your needs, and leave me to my plans."

He scowled at me, his sad demeanor having disappeared in a flash.

"Your plans… always your damned plans! You don't even know

what your plans are, anymore! You just go day to day, trying to figure out what to do next!"

I grabbed him by his throat, raising him off the floor. "What do you *expect* Thomas? Have you been through such a situation like this before? I think *not*. We may be in this together, but we have to work as a team. The more we fight against each other, the more we'll *lose*."

"Then stop fighting *me*, Anne!" He grabbed my wrist, trying to loosen my grip. I put him down, confused by what he meant.

In that second, Thomas grabbed me and crushed me to a wall, panting. An eager, hungry look in his eyes, he mashed his pelvis to mine, and I understood the reason for his sudden frenzy.

"Thomas--"

"No 'but's, *this* time, Anne. Stop fighting what you feel in your heart." He held my face and kissed me hard, his tongue tasting mine. "I must have you, or I'll *explode*," he whispered, his breath hot in my ear.

I let myself be distracted by this moment as he raised my skirt, picked up my leg, and wrapped it around his waist. He groped my thigh as he buried his face in my chest. I could feel him undoing his breeches with one hand, his manhood eagerly searching out my entrance before he found it, thrusting himself in with such a wanton ferocity, we both cried out in bliss.

Squish… squish… squish… squish…

We paid no attention to the noise as we lost ourselves in each other. Nothing else existed but that moment in time.

"God, how I've *missed* you," Thomas whispered, as he continued thrusting with a passion I so deeply craved. I gripped his hair as he grabbed my other leg. With a single hop, I wrapped my other leg around his waist, giving way to a deeper penetration on his part. He was rhythmic and wild, his gyrations sending me into a nirvana. As he engaged me in another deep kiss, I suckled his tongue, the sensations intense for him as he pushed himself deeper into me. I gasped, feeling a pleasurable pain deep within my womanhood. My fangs extended, and I plunged them into his neck. He grabbed my buttocks, intensifying the feel of his girth. I felt as though he would crush me right into the wall.

Squish… squish… squish… squish…

His lustful, heated poundings continued, as my womanhood took it all, consumed by my total abandon. When I managed to control my bloodthirsty cravings, it was Thomas' turn to return the favor.

The biting sensation was nothing like I had ever felt. So intimate, so profound... and sensually exhilarating.

A rivulet of blood went down my neck, which Thomas quickly trailed after with his tongue, then returned to the base point to finishing suckling.

A few more thrusts and he reached orgasm; his entire body stiffening as he let his manhood take over. I felt each throb of his release until the moment ebbed, and we panted in each other's arms in satisfaction.

Squish... squish... squish... squish...

I uncurled my legs from his hips, and I slowly slid down the wall as he fixed his breeches. My legs were sore and trembled from holding on so intensely, and I felt a little unstable standing on them. He smiled at me as his face glistened with perspiration.

Then, I looked over his shoulder, and my jaw dropped. Thomas noticed my expression, and very reluctantly, he turned his head to see what got my undivided attention.

What stood before us looked worse than anything we had ever encountered. It was a bloated, dripping, undead body. The clothing was torn and threadbare as it stuck to its skin. The skin itself was slimy and a pale shade of green, covered in putrid leeches, slugs, dead plant life, and larvae. Either it had no eyes, or they had been swollen shut, waterlogged. Its hair was matted, tangled with debris. The entire thing looked like it had been drudged up from the bottom of a lake... or worse.

We shrank back as this *thing* opened its mouth, bared its fangs, and lunged for us.

Thomas and I ducked, letting it slam against the wall, some of its flesh falling off on impact, and plopping to the floor. Unfazed, it turned, going after Thomas, as he was the closest. It grabbed him, so Thomas broke off its hand. Green water and dead insects poured from its mouth as it screeched. It hit Thomas with the one good hand it had left, sending him sailing backwards. Thomas landed on the floor with a thud, sliding a few yards on impact, and then it rounded on me next.

I grabbed a five-branched, table candelabra, and thrust it into this thing's body. Thick, black fluids drained from the wound. The candelabra went into the undead creature too easily, but despite its sopping, gelatinous body, I was amazed at its strength. It screeched again and stepped away from me, now trying to pull the candelabra out of its stomach.

"Dear *God*!" Thomas started. "It's *her*! The woman I fed from!"

"The same one I dumped in the creek," I concluded. "Cut off her head, Thomas, *quickly*!"

She must have understood what I said as she took off, her wet footprints leaving a trail of maggots and muddy sludge behind her. She didn't get far, as Thomas pulled his sword from his sheath in mid-run. With an angry roar, he sliced her head off with barely any effort. Her head landed with a pathetic-sounding splat, and her body dropped on the spot, more black muck leaking from her neck wound. He called for the rest of his troops to get rid of the foul thing by burning it, as he and I retreated to his quarters.

***

"It's definite, then. All undead creatures *must* be beheaded or burned to keep from returning," Thomas started.

"And there's still a few more to be captured -- unless they've multiplied since last time," I mentioned, shaking my head. "I didn't want this to happen! I didn't want to create more of our kind! I simply wanted to have my revenge, and end my torment."

"Which you still don't know how to do," Thomas said. "What if... your only way out *is* by beheading or burning? It'll still be as if Henry bestowed one of his predetermined punishments on you, anyway."

I sniffed and frowned. How truly ironic.

As I lay on his bed, he came over and sat beside me, running his fingers down the front of my corset, giving me a sly grin.

"I hope you had your fun," I started. "That won't happen again."

"Admit it, Anne! You loved it just as much I did." He raised my gown, ducking under it, and the next thing I knew, I felt his curly hair tickling my skin, and his head between my thighs.

I gasped. "Thomas... please... haven't you had enough?" I moaned, letting my head fall back as I felt his tongue venture into my womanhood with reckless abandon. He parted my thighs, exposing every inch of my folds to his wiles.

He brought his head back up, but only for a second. "Never," he answered with a puckish grin, returning to his mischievousness.

Thomas would not let up until he finally had his way -- making my body fall into a fit of spasms as I climaxed. He gently bit the inside of my thigh, suckling a small amount of my blood again, which made me collapse onto his pillow, relishing the intensity of the feeling. He kissed my womanhood and emerged from underneath my gown, still grinning.

"You'd have to be mad to say you haven't missed *that*," he answered, and I threw another one of his pillows at him in reply.

***

The next few nights, I continued my torturing of Henry again, impersonating Jane's voice at all hours, doing no more than calling his name or asking one simple question: *"Why"*. That question was part of my grand finale that he would be seeing soon enough. I'd watch as Henry would fall into fits of insanity, running around the room, looking everywhere, calling for Jane to show herself, or simply ball up into a fetal position while in bed, and cover his head with his pillow and scream or sob in misery.

Because of my cruelty, I expected to see Jane's ghost roaming the corridors of Whitehall next, wanting to stop me from doing such evil deeds to him. But, I never saw her. For all I knew, she *could* have been roaming the palace without my knowing, seeing that the spectral world was experienced so differently for all of us *un*-living folk. I would never know for sure.

Thomas and his troops were still having trouble tracking down the last of the undead women, and each day without finding them only made their trail colder and colder. Reluctantly, I gave in to the notion that more of my kind *would* survive after all, plaguing humanity for eternity, just as I feared. It was not a pleasant thought, and I hated the idea of being the cause of it. Had I been alive, never would I have allowed such creatures to exist.

Then, another grave day came for Henry. Charles was suffering a relapse, and was back in bed. Infection was spreading, and the physicians found it disturbing that such infection had lain 'quiet' within him for as long as it had. The Duke's diet had also been poor; swallowing was not something he still felt comfortable doing, as it often brought him pain --

and the physicians mentioned this also could have attributed to his sudden illness.

The wound they had sutured was beginning to ooze and leak pus. Charles' neck was starting to swell and discolor, so they had to drain the wound from time to time, and redress it with clean bandages. He was also running a high fever, and suffered from chills and night sweats.

Now it was Henry's turn to be at Suffolk's bedside. He begged and pleaded with the Duke and to God for him to get well, as he did not want to lose his best friend and confidante to the cold, uncaring will of death.

I slowly paced their room, watching the two of them -- Henry kneeling at his bedside while he prayed for him. To shake them up a bit, I blew out all the candles that were near the Duke's bedside, and Henry jumped.

"Away with you, demon! You will not take Suffolk from me!"

"*Empty words*," I whispered, and Henry made a feeble noise of fear and brandished a knife, swinging it every which way. I covered my mouth, trying not to laugh, as I wanted to keep the current scene more eerie and dramatic.

It took me a while to notice, but as I continued teasing Henry, the Duke seemed to be following my every move. I left Henry to his puffed-up ramblings about trying to kill the 'foul demon', and made my way to Charles' bed.

His eyes were locked on mine, and they widened the closer I got to him. I approached his bedside and bent over, peering into his face. We were nearly nose-to-nose.

"So, you *are* able to see me, Brandon," I said softly, and he gave a pained nod.

"Go... away... *witch*," Charles whispered, his breathing very labored.

I stood up, a hand now to my chin, rubbing it in thought.

I decided to leave his room, a new plan forming. Before I left, I whispered to Henry,

"*Stop now, you silly king, and tend to your friend.*"

He gasped again, looking all around himself in the room, before rushing to the Duke's bedside. To be derisive, I suddenly relit the candles for them, which gave Henry a bit of hope that Suffolk would be all right

after all.
>*Wrong.*

Chapter Nine

I deduced that the reason why Suffolk could see me was that he was near the brink of death, which made me continue pondering the world of the un-living. Suffolk was not quite dead -- still here on earth -- and could *see* me. Perhaps something to do with me being so earthbound allowed him to. Maybe that could explain my reason for seeing Smeaton, as he was earthbound, like me. And perhaps Katharine allowed herself a moment to come down to my 'plane of existence' so I could face her for that brief moment. That could also explain why Jane was able to see her just before she died, as well.

And maybe… if Jane truly was a ghost now, and I could not see her, perhaps she was on a plane so high, there was no reason for her to come down here. She didn't *need* to. She gave Henry what he so badly desired. Her work was done.

And if she *was* on a higher plane, did that mean she was that much *closer* to being with God? And if she was close to God… and I was here, still *earthbound*…

It felt as if the blood in my veins had frozen, and I immediately stopped myself from going further with my theological thinking. Sometimes I got carried away, and usually not for the better. They always veered towards darker, more despondent things.

Charles' misery continued for a few more days. I swear he must have been dragging out his final moments, for fear of what he would see on the other side. But alas, his sickly, ailing body could hold out no longer. Henry, his council, physicians, as well as I watched Suffolk's last moments as he struggled for air, his breathing sparse, clutching onto the very last threads of his life -- not to mention his bed sheets-- fighting death with his last dying breath.

Henry broke out into tears at the Duke's bedside, clasping his cold, limp, dead hand as he cried out his name between sobs. One of the physicians put out his candle, a silent and symbolic announcement of his departure, and another gently took Brandon's hand from Henry, placing it over his lifeless chest. Henry tried to regain his composure as he stood up, and in that moment, I saw a large piece of 'the fight' leave Henry's eyes.

Henry and Charles had been very good friends in their youth, practically like brothers. They did many things together and shared in the same interests. He was like family to Henry, and now he was no more…

…For now.

Charles Brandon, the Duke of Suffolk, had a luxurious and opulent ceremony in his name, which Henry paid for, naturally. Hundreds attended the service, which was held in Windsor at St. George's Chapel. It was so grand; one would have believed it was a wedding rather than a funeral, if not for the casket in plain view. Thomas had to stand at attention with the rest of the council, so Smeaton kept me company as we stood in the back of the church.

"He was a good fellow," Smeaton said carelessly, until I shot him a look. He cleared his throat and corrected himself. *"Until* he caused you grief and participated in your demise, my dear Anne."

I smirked at him, not saying a word.

Everyone who attended the service got one final chance to view his body before it would be laid to rest. I waited until everyone paid his or her last respects, before I walked up to Charles' coffin, and placed a small sprig of heather inside his coat. They did well in hiding the horrible gash on his neck. The huge, frilled collar of his shirt covered it. I looked at him for a moment, and then I leaned over and whispered in his ear.

"Hear me, Charles Brandon, and hear me well. I command you to come when I call to you. You will come to me, and you will obey my every command. I charge you with this, and you shall have no rest until you complete the task I give to you."

Thomas was aghast as I mockingly patted Charles' chest and grinned before leaving the chapel.

***

"That was utterly blasphemous, Anne… *utterly blasphemous*," Thomas whispered to me in a harsh tone when he found me in court later that evening. The hall was solemn as everyone conversed amongst themselves, most of the talk about Brandon's hey-day. Henry sat in his chair, more glum and withdrawn than ever. I feared he would lose all sense and sanity before I got the chance to finish my plans for him.

"It's not like I made him sit up in his coffin or anything," I shot back. "I merely whispered my goodbyes to him and patted his chest.

There's no harm in that."

"Whispered your *goodbyes*?" Thomas eyed me suspiciously and frowned. "You're going to do something horrible to him, I know it. Thank God you can't turn him into one of us."

"Even if I had the chance to, I'd never waste my time doing that to *him*," I answered in a nonchalant tone, trying to wave him off. "Go and comfort the king. It looks like he needs it."

"Trying to shoo me away now, are you?"

"As a matter of fact, *yes*."

Thomas balked, and then made his way over to the king in a huff, glancing back at me once. I gave a crooked grin before I took off.

At St. George's, I found Charles' resting place, circling his grave with more sprigs of heather as I continued to chant the same command I gave him at his service. Then, I returned to Whitehall. I would give him a bit of a resting period before I called him -- he was going to need it.

***

It was three days before I returned to his gravesite. The heather had long since wilted and dried, but that did not matter. I used the heather only to keep Charles earthbound.

With a fresh sprig of the flower in my palm, I closed my fingers around it, crushing it as I performed my summons.

"Charles Brandon, I command you to awaken, and rise from your grave. I command you to come forth, and do my bidding! Arise, Charles Brandon, and answer your mistress. You will obey me, and obey me now..."

It was only a minute before I felt a slight rumbling sensation in the ground directly under my feet. The rumbling grew more intense until I could see the grass shifting and moving, as if something underneath was pushing its way upward. I clawed away some of the dirt to ease Charles' efforts.

An arm and a head protruded from the ground first, dirt cascading from his hair. I grabbed his wrist and pulled him forward, more dirt raining into his casket. He smelled foul, but was in a much better condition than any of the other dead people I summoned before him. Henry made sure Suffolk had a well-tailored coffin, and it really did do its job of preserving him for as long as it had.

Charles' eyes looked opaque, his irises hazed over like a blind man's. His skin looked waxen and gray, his face sunken in, anorexic, the gash on his neck leaking again, as the front of those once-white ruffles of his collar were a nasty shade of yellow, and wet. His clothing was still in very good condition, again, thanks to his well-made coffin. Dirt was under his brittle, yellowed fingernails, and there were stains on his breeches, probably from his body expelling the last of the fluids he had left in his body.

He stood before me, silent, waiting on my command. I gave him a big grin. Charles' stare was so far away, it made chills run down my spine.

I leaned into him and whispered in his ear. Without hesitation, he turned and walked away, with Whitehall Palace as his destination, leaving a trail of sod in his wake.

***

Henry was in his private study, appearing as if he were deep in thought. He was fiddling with a quill, staring at a blank piece of parchment. I knew Henry was not fond of writing letters, so it surprised me he was attempting to scribble something. However, whatever thoughts he had, they were eluding him. He ran his hand through his hair in frustration, put the quill down, and simply folded his arms, staring off into nowhere. Good. As long as he stayed in there, I could bring in my little surprise for him.

Things had quieted down in the castle, and the evening was coming to a close. At this point, I did not care who saw Charles' walking corpse -- people would be too afraid to stop him, much less *approach* him.

Suffolk's pace seemed a little better than George's did; more than likely because he was not in the ground as long as my brother was. As I walked alongside him, Charles was very focused on his objective -- well, as focused as any undead being could be. His eyes were the most frightening. So blank, so colorless, so lifeless...

...So *dead*.

Although it did not matter who saw him, I still think I would have preferred a more stealthy attack. But, you cannot hide an undead being, and they have no will of their own to hide themselves. A woman spotted him from a distance, but paid him no mind at first. I *really* wished she had taken a different corridor, but no, she kept approaching us. When she finally realized who it was -- and his rather startling appearance, she let out a shriek. I pounced on her and broke her neck in order to silence her. Not being able to see me, I took her by surprise with minimal effort.

I was sure someone might have heard her, so I urged Brandon to pick up the pace. We were almost to Henry's study.

Once we were at his door, I made Charles wait outside. I entered first, my footsteps quiet. I got close enough to Henry that I softly blew in his ear. It was *too* soft, as he did not even notice; he was so deep in thought. I blew harder -- a single, forceful puff. He jumped, almost falling out of his chair, and produced an object from out of his doublet.

This time, he was holding a crucifix out in front of him. I guessed he finally realized a religious object would have been a better defense against a demon than a knife. I chuckled to myself, and he heard it. A bead of perspiration rolled down his temple, as he looked around frantically.

"Back, demon," he spat. "Away with you. Leave my castle! In the name of Our Lord Almighty, I *demand* you leave this castle!"

I tsk-tsked at him. "Poor Henry," I said. "Poor, *stupid* Henry."

"How dare you talk to me that way!" he continued, not even looking in my direction. I almost chuckled to myself again. "I am the King of England! I *demand* respect!"

"I care not who you are," I retorted. "And I respect no adulterers or heretics."

Getting the location of my voice right this time, he whipped around, finally facing in my general direction, the crucifix still thrust at arm's length.

"I banish you from my castle, demon! Be gone, foul creature!"

"Trying to be your own Pope?" I asked snidely. "That will not work on me."

"AWAY WITH YOU!" he bellowed, a vein in his forehead popping out. "I will *not* take this madness anymore!"

"You will take whatever I give you," I whispered, and with a thought, commanded Charles to enter the study.

Brandon stood in the doorway, unmoving for a moment. Again, I commanded him to come forward. Henry began whimpering and sweating even more.

"Ch-Charles? No...... no...... NOOOOOO!"

Brandon did not answer, only proceeded to walk towards Henry with a slow, unnerving, calculated pace. There was nowhere for Henry to run.

A bit of soil fell from Charles' hair, and the very first maggot I had seen since I resurrected him squirmed out of his ear and dropped onto his shoulder. I half-wondered if he had a head *full* of worms. Henry lost his voice, emitting only choked up sounds as his eyes widened in terror, while Charles' pale, dead, unfeeling blank ones stared back at him. Henry continued holding out his crucifix, but seeing it had no effect on him, dropped it, and brandished his knife once again.

Charles thrust his arms forward, following Henry as he made his way around the table, trying to keep himself separated from his dead friend. Suddenly, Charles overturned it, making a beeline towards the king. He grabbed Henry by his throat and began to squeeze, bringing Henry to his knees. He managed to stab Charles in his chest, but Charles remained vigilant and unfazed by Henry's action, as brownish-black fluid poured out from the wound Henry made.

"Charles! *Charles*! BRANDONNNN!" Henry managed to say to him, before Charles' clammy hands squeezed harder.

"Kill him... kill him, Brandon! KILL HIM!" I demanded in his mind.

Henry tried prying Charles' hands from his neck, and gasped for air before speaking.

"Charles! Stop! It's Henry! Why are you doing this? We were good friends!"

"KILL HIM, Brandon! I command you to kill him!"

I do not know how it was possible, but it seemed as if Charles had gained a will of his own. His hands still around Henry's neck, he began to loosen his grip.

"Can't..." Charles managed to say, his voice gravelly and rough. A bit of dirt spilled from his mouth, and Henry shrieked in shock.

"I COMMAND YOU TO KILL HIM!" I screamed in his head, and Charles winced, letting go of Henry. Stumbling, Henry got up and backed away, holding his throat and gasping for air.

"I command you to kill Henry, Brandon! You will obey me!"

Charles clutched his head, trying to shut out the sound of my voice.

"DAMN YOU, BRANDON! KILL HIM NOW!" I screamed again in his head as loud as I could. Charles let out a roar of frustration, tearing the rotted flesh of his face. Henry screamed again before Charles took hold of his neck once more and dragged him to one of the large stained glass windows in the room. Charles broke it with his elbow, glass tinkling everywhere, and tried positioning Henry in front it, determined to shove him out of the window.

"THOMAAAAS!" Henry shrieked, as he struggled against his former friend. Henry was already leaning partly out of the window, grabbing the edges of its frame to prevent himself from falling. He tore one of his sleeves on a shard of glass, cutting his skin.

Footsteps fast approached, and Thomas appeared in the doorway, stunned by the scene before him. He looked at me, then to Charles, and then to Henry.

"Get... him... *off*!" Henry sputtered, gasping again.

Grimacing, there was only one thing Thomas could do to end this horrid farce. He drew his sword, swung, and sliced off Brandon's head.

It tumbled to the floor and rolled, spilling hundreds of maggots about. A pool of larvae rained on Henry from Charles' neck wound and he screamed, pushing Brandon's body off him and right out of the window.

The three of us watched as Charles' body plummeted to the ground, and broke apart as easily as a China doll. Henry sank to the floor, a mess of tears and sobs. He covered his face, wailing in disbelief. Four more guards rushed into the room.

"What happened, Sir Thomas?" one of them asked.

He sighed before speaking. "It seems as if the devilry around the castle is continuing," he answered, sliding me a look, as I kept silent. "Something... *happened*... to Charles Brandon."

"But, the Duke is *dead*!" said another.

"Exactly," Thomas answered, pointing with his sword to the head on the floor. Charles' grisly, emotionless white eyes stared back at them, black worms wiggling out of his gaping mouth. The guards talked amongst themselves in nervous fervor.

"He attacked the king," Thomas continued. "Now, we must properly dispose of the body, and quickly, before anyone notices."

One guard reluctantly wrapped Charles' head in his cape, stepping on some of the maggots, popping them underfoot. The lingering three rushed out of the castle to get the remaining pieces of Brandon.

Thomas helped Henry up and sat him in a chair. Henry was hyperventilating, wide-eyed, slipping fast into madness. He stared into nothing, mumbling Charles' name repeatedly. Thomas was deathly afraid to do it, but he lightly slapped Henry's cheek to bring him around. Seeing it did not work -- and greatly relieved about that -- he shook Henry instead.

"Your Majesty... Your Majesty!" Thomas said in his ear. Henry snapped out of it, and looked at him.

"Thomas," he said, lowering his head. "That... that was *Charles*."

"I'm afraid so," he answered.

Henry looked to the maggots, immersed in the moonlight. Some of them were dead, and some were still wriggling about, slowly dying for lack of a warm place to hide and grow in.

"Did... did I bury him *alive,* Thomas?" He clutched at Thomas' doublet with a pained look on his face. "Did I bury him alive... and he went *mad* for it? My dear friend... my *best* friend... and I buried him *alive!*"

Thomas winced as he patted the king's shoulder, allowing him to believe the theory he just developed as the reasoning behind Brandon's resurrection. Poor Henry, still trying to keep such despicable events as logical as possible. Thomas glanced over to me again, his look full of resentment. I paid neither one of them any mind as I watched the guards below, running about like crazed, little worker ants, picking up parts of Charles' body and placing them in a dray cart. A dray cart, of all things! I nearly laughed at them, but stayed silent for the king's sake. I needed him to regain his sanity again so I could deliver the last and final blow. I *had* considered sparing him of my 'Jane plan' by using Charles as my weapon instead, but since that idea was now foiled, it was back to my 'Jane plan' again.

Leaving Thomas and Henry to themselves, I ventured outside to where the guards were. They were still fussing about, not sure of what to do with the body parts once they put them on the cart.

There was still a splay of intestines and other innards on the ground, blackened and discolored pieces of his liver, lungs and kidneys.

"What will we do with *this* mess?" one guard asked, hands on his hips as he looked at them.

"Let the dogs have at it, if they want it," said another. "I'm not picking it up. If the dogs don't get it, the ravens certainly will."

My stomach turned at the thought.

"Good God in heaven!" a voice exclaimed from behind me. I knew it was Smeaton before I even looked. "Remind me to *never* get on your bad side!"

"I didn't do that to Charles. His body fell out of the window right after Thomas cut his head off."

"Cut his--?" Smeaton stopped himself. "Never mind. Spare me the details."

"Gladly. Seeing the impact alone would have made one vomit."

"And if I *had* a stomach, I would have done just that, right *now*." He stared at Charles' innards strewn around the site. "So... are you through with your hellish revelry, Anne?"

I paused for a moment. Should I let things be? Had I felt as if I tortured Henry enough?

Still, he did not realize it was *I* who brought him into this personal hell of mine. I was merely the 'mystery woman' who roamed the corridors of Whitehall Palace.

I turned to Smeaton, sniffed, and tilted my head up. "No," I said firmly. "He *will* come to know me again. But first..." I paused. "I want to take a trip to bedlam."

Smeaton tilted his head in wonder.

***

At first, I had been happy that Cromwell landed himself in the asylum, but after a while, it became a small, nagging thought in the back of my mind. Him being there wasn't enough. Cromwell was still *alive*, and that left me dissatisfied with his outcome. I wanted him *dead*.

Smeaton followed me, merely curious as to what I had planned for him. Even *I* still had no clue as to what I would do, and muddled through a couple of ideas. My first one was to have him hang by one of his own bed sheets from the rafters of the building. *That* would surely be a mystery to all indeed, especially if I put him so high and in such a way that they would have no idea *how* he was able to hang himself there in the first place. I nearly chose that plan, but after what I had done to him at the

Tower, it would almost feel like I was repeating myself. I wanted to do something *different*. On the other hand, I could torture him a bit more and give him a simple chase that would certainly drive him insane, and maybe incorporate a few undead fiends to join in. I decided on my second idea. In addition, since Smeaton was with me, I knew he would love to join in on the fun once more. I was glad he had no qualms with anything I did. Thomas was becoming more and more of an emotional burden, and it was starting to grate on me.

If I did not know any better, I would swear bedlam was just as horrendously kept as a typical dungeon -- minus the torture devices, filthy straw, and bloodstains everywhere. Even so, nothing about the building invoked a sense of cleanliness. The walls were bleak, gray and dingy, the people within half as dirty as a typical prisoner. Sanitation was sorely lax in this place.

Since Smeaton was a ghost, and I was already in my invisibility guise, we had no problems with getting into the compound. A large bit of land was fenced off for the poor unfortunate folks of the place to wander around in, and wander they did. They all were clothed in nothing more than their dressing gowns. Some of them talked to themselves or to things that were not there. But for all I knew, perhaps they *were* talking to someone. Now I began to doubt that these types of people were insane after all.

Some were in much of a worse condition than the 'talkers' were, however. Some sat huddled against trees, playing with dirt, insects, even their own feces. I grimaced and continued on.

One elderly woman with scraggly, thinning hair walked aimlessly through the grass, barefoot, with fecal stains on her gown. She had a huge flower placed behind her ear. Smiling with her eyes closed and her head tilted towards the sky, she kept saying how much God loved her. I wanted to ponder over that, but my current mind frame was too focused on finding Cromwell.

A young man was going around the grass with his gown flipped up over his head, leaving the rest of his naked body exposed to the elements. He was making noises and waving his body about in slow motion. Perhaps he was pretending to be a ghost?

"Dear Lord," Smeaton said, looking at the sights. "So this is what bedlam is like."

"No surprise there as to why no one speaks of these places much," I replied. "Bedlam is where people put their unfortunates... to *forget* about them."

'Ghost Boy' stopped short, and flipped his gown back down, looking around himself. His eyes settled Smeaton and me. He kept looking back and forth between the two of us, then let out an ear-piercing scream before running in the opposite direction.

Smeaton and I looked at each other.

"Hmm... looks like the 'insane' have extra abilities regular people don't... like seeing the paranormal."

"Interesting..." I trailed off. Perhaps my earlier theory *was* correct.

We came across a heavy, wooden door that would lead us inside the building. I opened it slowly so it would not creak as much, as Smeaton trailed ahead of me, checking the place out.

The inside walls were just as dingy as the outside ones. There were lots of windows to let light in, but as of right now, many candles lit the place. I was also a bit surprised that the caretakers of the unfortunates were still letting the patients wander around outside in the dark. However, with the stone barrier surrounding the place, perhaps they figured they did not need to worry.

And speaking of the caretakers, where were *they*? I got my answer when we saw two of them in a secluded, sectioned off part of a room, satisfying their carnal urges. A young man sat in a chair while another man around his age straddled him. They rocked back and forth for a moment before he began bouncing his lover up and down on his hips while they moaned in pleasure.

"You have *got* to be kidding me," Smeaton said. "Getting your jollies in a place like *this*?"

"Lust cares not where it's at, when the need to quench it arises," I mumbled, thinking of Thomas' and my little romp, and we kept walking.

The patient rooms were very spartan -- windows, a bed, a chair, and a small table. The door windows were very generous, perhaps not wanting to let the patients feel like they were truly prisoners. Nevertheless, the windows still had bars.

As we progressed, we noticed some doors started to appear more prison like, and the rooms even more sparse, having only a mattress on the floor. The walls within these rooms were also filthy, smeared with foul-colored streaks that I could only guess at what they were. Some were occupied with people who sat balled up in a corner, some in shackles, some screaming and banging at their doors, or worse, banging their heads on the walls until they bled. Others tried reaching out through the bars on their windows, crying for help. A lot of them looked emaciated, with dirty, stringy hair, and animal-like expressions on their faces. There was no sense or civility in their eyes. Whatever happened to them, they had been stripped of their humanity in the process.

"Where the devil are they keeping Cromwell?" Smeaton asked me, and I shrugged my shoulders. I knew of one other bedlam, and wondered if he might have been in *that* one, instead. But, we would thoroughly investigate this place first, before jumping to another one.

We came upon a hallway that split in two directions. Smeaton and I parted to save time.

After a few minutes, it was Smeaton who got lucky, waving me down to his end. I was there in seconds.

Perhaps the king requested that Cromwell be given special treatment, as his room was different from all the others, even a bit larger. He was also allowed writing supplies. Cromwell was in bed, asleep, resting peacefully. His face even looked like he was stress free.

I sniffed. I could not allow him to stay that way.

Smeaton drifted through Cromwell's cell door. I opened it and walked in.

I bent over his sleeping form and shook him gently.

"Wake up, Cromwell," I said in a teasing, sing-song voice. "We have unfinished business, you and I."

Cromwell snorted, opened his eyes, and yelped, backing away from me. I gave a vicious grin.

He closed his eyes. "This isn't real… this isn't real…"

I sighed in boredom and sat down. "Do we *have* to go through this again? I'm very much here in your pathetic little room, Cromwell." I glanced at the table, noticing the papers he had scribbled on. It looked like it was a diary of some sort, and I scanned the pages.

"Ah, it looks as if you've written a tale of my resurrection," I said playfully, glancing from the pages to him. As I continued sifting through them, I noticed a sketch he did of me. Surprisingly, it was a good likeness, considering he was not fond of art in the least.

"Nicely done," I continued in my mocking tone, holding his sketch up beside my own face, grinning. "Don't you think?" I turned to Smeaton so he could get a look as well.

Cromwell looked confused as he watched my little gesture.

"Oh, Smeaton is here as well. Remember *him*, Cromwell?" I snapped, my playful act now dropped. "A perfectly *innocent* man you had tortured to *death*. Perfectly *INNOCENT*!" I threw his inkwell at him, hitting him in his forehead. It left a small, bloody cut, and he winced in pain.

"Mark Smeaton," he said, rubbing his wound. "He's *can't* be here!"

"On the contrary," I replied, and gestured to Smeaton to play something. His violin materialized in his hand, and he put it up to his chin, now playing a cheerful tune. Cromwell gasped, looking around his chambers, wondering where the sound was coming from. Then he covered his head, moaning in grief.

"Stop, please! *Stop!*"

That only provoked Smeaton to get closer to Cromwell, and he played right in Cromwell's ear. He jumped out of bed, and then, realizing he was too close to *me*, he made another jump towards his door. Noticing it was wide open, he looked to me, to the door, then to me again.

I waved him off, grinning. "You know you want to," I said, sounding rather blasé.

On that note, he took off.

Smeaton stopped playing and looked at me in surprise. "You're *letting* him get away?"

I snorted. "Please. I'm merely giving him the chance to *believe* he can get away." I took up his papers and burned them in a candle flame, dropping them to the floor, watching them as they blackened and curled as the fire consumed them.

I sighed and looked at Smeaton. "Well, I guess we should give chase now."

Smeaton grinned and followed me as I casually walked out of the building.

The patients were still wandering about as if nothing had happened. It wasn't as if any of them would try to *stop* Cromwell.

I scanned the grounds, trying to spot any quick movements, and then walked over to a tree, noticing something odd in its branches. I looked up and saw several bed sheets tied in knots, going over the compound's wall. Damn. Had I actually given him enough time to do *that* much? I laughed. He was actually trying to give me a challenge!

"See you on the other side of the wall," I told Smeaton, making a dash to bedlam's entrance and around the wall to where the tree was. I looked at the makeshift rope Cromwell had made and shook my head. Crafty old fart, he was. I now saw that desperation helped make one *very* ingenious when it came to escape.

Now there lay nothing but vast fields and woods front of us.

"Ready?" I asked Smeaton.

"Of course," he answered.

"Let's race to see who finds him first," I said with a smile, and both of us took off, laughing all the way.

***

Ten minutes had barely gone by before Smeaton came to me.

"I'm afraid I've won, Lady Anne," he announced, giving a graceful bow.

"Don't keep me in suspense," I answered with a chuckle. "Where is he?"

He pointed off in the distance. "He disappeared off into that patch of woods -- and there's also a potter's field out there as well." He winked at me.

"Perfect!" I exclaimed, making a dash towards the woods. "A potter's field means more bodies to resurrect, and more ways to torture the old fool."

Smeaton shivered. "I'll keep a bit of a distance while you do your handiwork."

As I walked through the woods, I found the graves, no more than twenty of them. Just enough to give Cromwell a really good scare.

I tapped on their headstones. "Arise, all of you! Arise and join me in my revenge!"

Moments passed, and I felt a rumbling under my feet. The grasses moved and pulsed as the bodies of the dead came forth. Amongst the undead were a few children, and for a second, my heart went out to those innocent beings, never allowed to live out their lives. Now they were hapless puppets in my little, ghastly game.

"Find Thomas Cromwell," I ordered them, and they lumbered off to locate their victim.

Having a brief moment to ourselves, I looked to the night sky, and asked Smeaton a question. "Are you getting tired, yet?"

He gave me an inquisitive look. "My Lady?"

"Are you getting tired. Of *this*." I gestured to the two of us as we began to stroll through the woods.

He paused for a while. "Sometimes I am, sometimes I'm not. I guess it all depends on my mood."

"I feel the same way. It's as if I can't make a firm decision." I leaned against a tree.

"Perhaps you'll be fulfilled once you finally deal with Henry."

"Perhaps," I answered, still sounding a bit unsure.

"What about Thomas?" he said, the name snapping me out of my little daze.

"Thomas?" I repeated. "I'm not sure I understand."

"Thomas is beginning to look a bit frayed around the edges, if you know what I mean."

I recalled the looks he gave me in Henry's study after he had to kill Charles, sending the Duke into the arms of death once again. "He's becoming more and more temperamental and moody." I sniffed, and then added wryly, "He should have become an actor instead of a councilman."

Smeaton laughed. "His plays and poetry *are* well crafted. You might be right, Anne."

Our casual conversation was abruptly broken when we heard a scream in the distance.

"A-ha!" Smeaton said. "I believe our fellow, friendly dead folk have found our target."

Not wanting to rush, I continued walking at a fast pace, not the quick, unnatural speed I had become used to. The longer Cromwell was tortured, the better.

He screamed again, and I grinned. Listening to his agony was quite pleasant.

I noticed the undead beings had Cromwell surrounded in a large, lopsided circle. No matter which way he ran, he came upon a dead person, and screamed again.

"Disband," I told them all in their minds, and slowly, they made an about face and shambled away.

Time for Smeaton and me to have our little fun.

I put myself in Cromwell's path, and stepped out from behind a tree. He yelped and turned around, running away from me. He came to an open field and made a mad dash through the clearing. I sighed.

"Boring," I mumbled, walking out of the woods.

Ahead of me, I heard Smeaton's violin suddenly play, and Cromwell stopped short, falling down, disappearing into the grass. Smeaton now stood where Cromwell had fallen, and waved me over.

The field grasses were getting higher and higher, making them difficult to walk through, but I casually continued onward.

Cromwell stood up and watched me approach him. A heavy breeze picked up; making the grasses sway as my cloak billowed in the wind and the hood fell away. My hair blew wildly around my head.

"DEMON! WITCH!" he yelled at me, wide-eyed, running again.

I rolled my eyes in annoyance. Time for this chase to be done and over with.

With my uncanny speed, I appeared in his path, and he almost knocked me over. He gasped, backing away from me, begging for mercy. Smeaton flanked him. When Cromwell turned in Smeaton's direction, he screamed again. Smeaton must have made himself materialize just enough that Cromwell could finally see him.

Cromwell took off in another direction, but he did not get far.

None of us noticed that we were just a few yards away from a cliff.

It was as if Cromwell was there one second, and gone the next -- except we heard him screaming for the last and final time.

Smeaton and I rushed over to where he had disappeared, and looked down. His arms and legs flailing in mid air, unable to escape his fate, Cromwell plummeted to his doom. He landed head first, dashing his head upon the jagged rocks below, his body broken and mangled, limbs askew in all sorts of unnatural angles. A spray of grayish-red matter had exploded from his skull, and Smeaton actually heaved, which I found amusing.

"Damn it," I said to myself, looking at the scene below. "Well, that ends that."

Smeaton, weak in the knees, collapsed to the ground in a daze. "I don't want to see brains again, Anne. Brains are not meant to be seen *outside* of one's head."

I smirked, helping him up. It felt good to actually *feel* him for a change. He gave me a hug before settling back into his spectral form.

"That took quite a bit out of me," he started. "Too bad I can't do that for lengths at a time. Still, the power of one's will is a mighty thing!"

I looked over the cliff again. "I guess he'll be food for the carrion crows, now."

Smeaton made a face. "Oh well. At least they'll have a fine breakfast come morning!"

I made a noise of disgust, but couldn't help but give a tiny grin.

"Really, Mark, sometimes I don't know who's more melodramatic, you, or Thomas."

***

Our trip back to the castle was a gloomy one. Tonight was a night for ghosts, it seemed. All over England's hills, we saw many specters floating aimlessly about, no doubt the remnants of the Pilgrimage and the wars that came before it. A sad sight, indeed. Even the soil itself seemed haunted, possessed by the same phantom energies -- and I had no doubt that it *was*. The trees themselves now seemed like lone, ominous sentinels that burst forth from under the ground, their huge, skeletal branches clawing at the sky, reaching for something unknown to us. Despite it being a clear, cloudless night, the lands looked darker than usual, even in the moonlight.

"It feels so… unsettling," I said. "The murkiest depths of England have become unleashed."

"And shall always remain. There's too much bloody history seeped into her very veins that cannot be erased."

"Including our own, Smeaton… including *our own*," I replied sadly, as we pushed onward.

***

We arrived at Whitehall Palace, with a few hours of night left to spare. It was deathly silent, since everyone had gone to bed.

"Well, that was some dreadfully delightful fun, my dear Anne! Thank you for such a thrilling romp!" Smeaton said with a smile. "And now, I shall return to my rounds. I shall see you anon?"

I nodded, and Smeaton dematerialized, his melodic music once again resonating throughout the castle.

I felt reluctant to return to Thomas' chambers. I was not sure if I would see the loving, caring Thomas, or the foreboding, surly and dour one.

As I opened his chamber door, a knife that struck into the wood -- just inches from where my face would have been -- greeted me. I scowled at him, and he returned the expression.

"I guess this means you *don't* want to talk," I said coldly, and slammed his door shut, walking away.

I trembled in anger. Damn him! I hated when he made me feel so conflicted with my feelings for him! His emotions blew hot and cold just as much as Henry's!

He opened his door.

"Damn you, Anne! Come back!" he whispered harshly.

I whipped around, "No, Thomas. Just… stay away from me right now."

He padded up the hallway in his bare feet, his steps muffled by the carpeting. I continued to ignore him until he grabbed my arm. I looked down at his hand, then to him, sneering. Getting the message, he let me go.

"I'm sorry," he said stiffly. "I--I don't know what came over me."

"You know *very well* what came over you," I snapped, continuing onward. "And I know you're not sorry, so your apology means *nothing* to me."

He trailed after me. "Anne--"

"Our relationship is *poisonous*, Thomas," I said, stopping again. I looked him long and hard in his eyes. "There's nothing there, can't you see that? We'll be drowning in each other's hatred for each other before we know it. More and more of your new personality sheds off your old one, exposing how you truly feel. There's nothing for us anymore, Thomas, I *told* you. There never *will* be."

"I don't want to hear this, Anne," he said, grabbing my hand in a pleading manner. "I don't want to lose what we have!"

"What we *had*, Thomas, what we *had*! What we have *now* is *nothing*! It is a twisted, perverted, unnatural *thing* that we share. Something that I know in my heart won't be permanent." I wrenched my hand out of his grip. "And besides, you can't always have what you desire." I continued walking.

"Anne, please don't do this to us… not again!"

I turned back around. "I never separated us the *first* time! Get it straight, Thomas, before I have a mind to torture *you* as well!"

"You'd have a hard time of it, considering we're on even ground." He had the audacity to give me a wicked, half-grin that looked the slightest bit threatening.

"You *bastard*," I hissed. "Just remember who made you what you are!" I spat, and sped off.

***

I could not believe how quickly Thomas was turning on me. Alas, evil has no heart, so it was to be expected eventually. The thought of possibly having to kill him nearly broke my heart.

I was not going to worry about that now. I decided to peek in on the king, and see how he was holding up.

Sneaking into his chamber, I found it interesting that Henry was still clutching onto Jane's wedding gown, having a very fitful rest.

It was nearing dawn, so I had decided to wait a few nights before I started in on Henry's demise, and looked upon a different place to rest for the day. I headed to Hever Castle, knowing it would be completely dissolved.

I knew it had become property of The Crown by now, but as long as no one was residing in it yet, I could still call it home.

Hever looked black and desolate under the moonlight. Just a looming heap of stone and mortar, destined to weather away over time, just like anything else in this world that was made by man.

Inside was just as cold as ever. I looked at the fireplace, getting dusty from lack of use. My footsteps echoed through the room as I looked around. I did not know why I decided to come back to this place to rest. I could honestly say there was truly nothing here to come back to. Perhaps I was torturing myself with my own ghosts of the past.

I went up the stairs and reached my bedroom, surprised that many of the furnishings remained. I sat on my bed, running my hands across the blankets. I lay down next, took a deep breath, and allowed myself to fall asleep.

I saw myself in lush fields of green. The sun was high in the sky. The air was warm. I was dressed in my finest damask, with colors of rose and teal. I was laughing and spinning in the open lands, delirious with joy. George was as handsome as ever, bringing to me a huge bouquet of daffodils. I smiled as I took them and gave him a kiss on his cheek.

My father stood off to the side, smiling at me as well, twirling a single daffodil between his fingers. And Thomas, and Smeaton! They were sitting on the grass, a huge picnic spread out on the ground before them on a large blanket, beckoning me to join them.

I called after George and my father to join us at the picnic. I dropped to my knees, reaching over and taking a sweetcake. It tasted so heavenly... and the assorted fruits -- cherries, apples, peaches! I took a sprig of grapes, popping a few into my mouth, relishing their sweetness.

I watched as all the men in my life that I so dearly loved and cared for sat with me, eating, talking, and laughing, enjoying the day with me. Everything was so right, so *perfect*, just like how it was supposed to be... just like how I *wanted* it.

But then, something odd happened. Father crushed the daffodil he had in his hand, giving me a hard look. I felt my heart race in anxiety as I looked at the rest of the men around me.

A thin red mark suddenly appeared around George's neck. He clutched his throat, and then his head fell from his neck, dropping into the pile of food before us. Then the same thing happened to Smeaton. I was screaming, my heart racing. Blood was everywhere. Thomas was now dressed in prisoner's rags, as was my father. The food was spoiled, rotten and brown, insects and maggots crawling all over it.

I looked down at my dress, noticing it was the same one I was executed in. I felt a burning sensation around my neck, and struggled against a suffocating feeling.

That's when I gasped and woke up.

I sat up in bed, and for a fleeting moment, I thought I had a bad dream. That everything was fine and as it should have been. Then a sinking feeling washed over me, telling me not to be so foolish.

I walked over to my mirror, dreading the worst.

I stared at my pale reflection, my red eyes staring back at me, my black locks streaked with white.

I covered my face and wailed as I crumpled to the floor.

***

It was dusk when I awoke, still on the floor, and feeling miserable. I smoothed my hair back, listening for sounds, making sure no one had entered my former home. Sighing, I got up. Seeing my reflection again, I hit the mirror, shattering it into little pieces.

A funny thing, life was. Was it hundreds of little random acts of chance, or were they perfectly laid out for each and every one of us? Was it *meant* for my parents to meet, and have Mary, my brother and me? Was it *meant* for my father to serve the Tudors as much as he had, and have a sudden desire to rise to power so much that he would be so willing to ruin the lives of his two daughters to obtain it? Was it meant for me to become Queen of England, only to die within three years of my reign? Was it meant for me to curse my days and curse my God, only to wind up existing as this horrible creature with a dark and twisted lust for revenge and blood? Surely, something like this could *not* be in God's design! Then, I thought back to what Thomas mentioned -- that becoming this creature probably *was* part of God's grand design. If that was true, then it seemed like a cruel joke! What *was* His design? And what sense did becoming this unholy thing make? What purpose would my being this creature *fulfill*? And *if* all this was meant to be, was I still following the so-called path that was laid out before me? So many questions I did not have the answers for, and could not understand. Perhaps, I too, was a puppet in someone else's grander scheme of things.

Not feeling like waxing philosophical, I cast my thoughts aside. I did not need to make myself any more insane than I already was.

I stood up, straightened my gown and cloak, and looked at my fractured reflection before I walked out of my room.

My fractured reflection. I sniffed at the irony. I was way *beyond* being fractured.

***

I returned to Whitehall when court was at its busiest, so I could blend in with the crowds. Henry was not present again. I had given him a tough night to deal with previously, so no wonder there. And since I did not see Thomas, I had a feeling he was with the king. Let him. It was obvious that he made his decision. He sided with my enemy, and so I would have to treat *him* like one as well.

I was sure Henry would be either in his study or in his chambers, so I checked the study first and found it empty. I made my way to his bedroom next.

As I rounded a corner, I got a whiff of a fragrance. Frankincense. That was odd. Usually such a precious scent was reserved for religious ceremonies. I wondered what was going on.

The scent grew heavier the closer I got to his chamber door. It got to the point where it became stifling, and I could barely breathe. Another oddity. I had no problems with such a scent when I was alive, so why was it bothering me now?

Silly question. I knew the answer the moment I thought of it.

The more I inhaled, the weaker I felt. I found it amazing how this holy scent had such an awful affect on me. I made an about face and began a quick pace away from Henry's door. As soon as I got to the end of the corridor, I leaned against the wall, gasping for breath.

Then Thomas appeared out of nowhere.

He grabbed me by my throat and shoved me against the wall. Having no time to react, he forced a kiss on me as I tried squirming my way out of his grip. He bit my lip before stepping back, and I wiped my mouth, pulling away red tinged fingers. I looked at him in shock.

The look in his eyes was not kind as he gave me a pointed grin.

"I'd watch myself, Anne, if I were you," he said in a sinister tone, walking down the hallway towards the king's chambers. Rubbing my throat, I watched in astonishment as he entered Henry's chambers, the frankincense having no affect on *him* at all!

Damn this curse! How unfair and one-sided it was!

Then I paused, recalling his immediate words to me.

Thomas threatened me. *Again.*

When I killed him, there would be no love lost between us.

***

I waited an hour before venturing back to Henry's chambers. The frankincense had worn off. I was trying to push open his door, which, for some odd reason, was damp to the touch. Then all of a sudden, it felt like the wood was *burning* me. What in God's name was going on *now*?

My flesh felt singed as I pulled away, tendrils of smoke drifting from my palms and fingertips up into the air. I gasped and backed away from the door. I shook my hands, trying to cool them down.

Thomas was standing behind a nearby suit of decorative armor, a low-sounding, devious chuckle coming from him.

"I doused His Majesty's entire door with holy water," he said, sounding cocky. "I figured; why not give it a shot? Just like with the frankincense. *Anything* that might work against an unholy creature is worth testing."

I narrowed my eyes. Meddlesome little bastard.

He started coming towards me, and I hissed at him.

"Thomas, I'd advise you not to come near me." I was trembling in anger again. Not a nice feeling.

He sniffed, ignoring me.

"If you even *dare* to come within a few paces of me, it's best you have a weapon of some sort to kill me with, or I swear I'll kill you *first*," I continued, my eyes glowing a brighter shade of red.

He stopped in his tracks as if thinking it over, and then went into the king's chambers briefly, returning to the hallway with a sword in hand.

Bold as brass, as usual.

Henry poked his head out of the door, and his eyes widened when he saw me.

"The mystery woman!" Henry blurted, and then looked over to Thomas, whose gaze was solidly fixed on me.

"Let's end this," he growled.

"I agree," I answered, then ran towards him, screeching.

I had no intentions in playing fair. I charged at him with unnatural speed and slammed my whole body right into him before he could strike. He flew backwards, landing on the floor with a thud.

He jumped up and shook it off, returning the same attack move. I collided with the armor and fell, metal clanging loudly around me. Damn it! That was the second time that happened to me! Now I was *really* annoyed.

As I got up, he came towards me again, brandishing the sword. I reacted quickly, grabbing the sword that was part of the armory and getting behind him in one swift movement. I held the blade up to his neck, and he froze, keeping still.

"I wonder what you'd look like -- *a head shorter*," I asked mockingly with a smirk.

"I wondered the same thing about *you*," he retorted, rounding on me and stabbing me in my midsection.

I shrieked and quickly handed his move right back to him, except I twisted the sword, making it more difficult for the wound to close. He gasped, and then coughed, blood sputtering from his mouth as he dropped to his knees, looking at me with such an expression of shock and confusion. Did he *not* expect me to defend myself from him, despite him being an old flame? Ha!

"*Thomas*!" Henry yelled as I stumbled off, pulling the sword out of me and dropping it to the floor as I made my getaway.

"I'll see you *burned*, woman!" Henry called after me as he knelt by Thomas' side. "Guards! Get the physicians!"

I was now twice injured. Three times would be the charm. Perhaps my last one would give me rest from this madness.

***

It looked so strange to me. It was as if Thomas was taking Charles' place as Henry's right-hand man. He stuck to Henry's side like a barnacle to a boat. If this was Thomas' idea of protecting the king from me, it was surely a bad one.

It took me a whole night to recuperate from my accident, and I emerged from my new hiding place in the deepest part of the dungeon, which Smeaton had found for me. I would not have to worry about anyone finding me *there*.

Henry was looking more and more sickly, but his ailments did not make me feel an ounce of sympathy for him. Not after what he had done to me, my family, and those closest to me.

I recalculated my immediate plans. Since I could not get anywhere near Henry for now, I would simply have to work my magic from afar.

No one could see me in my invisibility guise except Thomas and Smeaton, and Thomas could see Smeaton as well. There *had* to be a way to divert Thomas away from the king!

Oh well. Desperate times called for desperate measures.

I led a young woman of the court away from the crowds, bit her, drained her until she was too weak to have a will of her own, and then commanded her to 'attack' Henry's men.

I shoved her back into the crowd, weak, disheveled and bewildered. Her neck wounds were draining remnants of her precious life fluid. Other people began to notice her, pointed, and talked. She ignored them all as she stumbled her way towards the king. The closer she got to him, the more feral she began to look. Thomas and the guards were also noticing her odd behavior, and stood firm, as she was just a few yards away from them. She gave a vicious roar and bared her fangs, leaping forward and attaching herself to one of the men, knocking him down. She tried biting his face off as another guard tried to pull her off of the first one. People in court began to scatter in confusion and fear.

While the woman kept up the diversion, I watched to see where Thomas was taking Henry for safety, and followed after them. It looked to be another secret room I never knew of before. I heard Thomas say he was going to check on Henry's guards and to stay inside.

When Thomas left, I made my move.

I opened the door slowly, and peeked in. Henry stood beside a window, his arms folded, leaning his head against the wall.

"Oh my beloved Jane," he whispered, tears flowing down his cheeks. "I miss you *so* much. I wish you were here, and yet, I am glad you are not, for I would not want you to witness the maladies that plague your kingdom, the evils that run rampant. These things -- how they drive me to madness!"

Her kingdom?! I growled under my breath.

Now, let us see if this new bit of magic would work wonders for me.

I disguised myself in what I called a 'veil of illusion'. I envisioned the subject I wished to become, then willed myself to look exactly like it.

And my subject was *Jane*.

I removed my cloak, as it was too familiar to Henry now, but I wondered about the rest of my attire. I had been executed in the gown I wore, but I did not think he'd remember it, since he wasn't present at my hanging.

He did not hear me, which was good. I crept up to him until he sensed me. When he turned his head and looked at me, I would have given anything in the world to see him look at me the way he had, *once* upon a time.

"Jane," he whispered, inching his way to me. "Can this be?" He slowly extended his arm as he moved slowly towards me; as if afraid I would suddenly vanish. "My dear, beloved Jane! You are alive and well!"

"Not alive, Henry, but a ghost," I replied, smiling, and his expression melted into a pained look.

"My dear, sweet Jane!" he exclaimed. "You have no *idea* how *much* I miss you!"

I took a step backward. "If you miss me, then why did you let me die?"

Henry looked taken aback. "Let you die? Never!"

"Yes, Henry, *you let me die*. None of your physicians could help me. Why, Henry? *Why*? I died giving you a son; was that all you wanted me for? To give you an heir, then discard me like I was nothing?"

He dropped to his knees, his hands folded in a pleading manner. "Please, beloved wife! I would *never* discard you! I loved you with every fiber of my being! I loved you more than Katharine -- even Anne!"

Those words stung, and I frowned. Time to get more manipulative.

"You love nothing but yourself, Henry. You cared not whether I lived or died, as long as you got what you wanted! Your *heir*! You regard all your women as pawns, and I was a pawn as well!"

Henry kept shaking his head, the tears streaming down his face.

"No Jane, *no*! I *loved* you! Don't you understand? I LOVED YOU! You *must* believe me! I still cry for you *every* night! How I want you in my arms again! Please, please, have mercy on your husband, who still loves you so!"

I smirked. "All your power, Henry, and you couldn't save me from *dying*. Did you think I *wanted* to die?"

"God took you from me, Jane. I have not the power to stop Him. For the life of me, I'll never know why He chose to take you from me, but

I have not forgotten you, nor will I *ever*!"

I maneuvered my way towards the window. "Do you still wish to be with me, Henry?"

"Yes! If God would have me, then yes!"

"Do you truly love me, Henry?"

"Yes! *Yes*! You *know* I do!"

"Would you *die* for me, Henry?"

"*Anything*, to have you at my side again." He approached me, but still afraid to touch me.

"Really?" I brandished a small knife, and aimed for his chest.

Henry's eyes widened the moment I was about to strike, but someone tackled me to the floor.

"Damn you, Thomas!" I yelled, kicking him off of me. I hissed at him, still in my Jane guise, but baring my fangs and red eyes.

Henry made a long gasping noise that sounded like he was having a heart attack. Both Thomas and I looked at him.

"My Lord!" Thomas rushed over to him and sat him in a chair. In the few seconds it took for him to do that, I was already gone, having grabbed my cloak in my wake.

***

I was *furious*! I screamed and screamed throughout the corridors of Whitehall, tearing down banners, knocking over planters, armory, tables, *anything* that was near me that wasn't nailed down. I just *knew* I looked like a madwoman, carrying on like that.

Even Smeaton was reluctant to approach me. "My Lady!" he exclaimed, and when I turned, he was completely speechless for a moment.

"My Lady... *Jane*?" He looked around, hoping to see me. "Oh dear..."

Ugh! This illusion was lasting a bit longer than I wished. I looked at my reflection in a pane of glass, and laughed. To look like her -- save my red eyes and fangs -- really did a number on my mentality for a moment.

"It's only me, Smeaton," I said in my regular voice, and he gawped at me.

"*Anne*? Oh, Dear God -- what did you do to yourself?"

"I was trying to experiment a bit with my magic, and worked up an illusion spell. I wanted to look like Jane in order to torment the King some more."

"Well, you've really gone overboard this time," he answered, fondling a lock of my now blonde hair. He flinched and let it go. "Really... *really*... overboard."

"That damned Thomas stopped me from killing the king! *Again!*" I put my hands on my hips. "I was SO close!" I took a deep breath and exhaled, trying to calm down. "I need to get rid of him. He's become *such* a thorn in my side lately!"

Smeaton tapped a finger to his lips, thinking. "Poison?"

I smirked. "That's too predictable, Mark. His food is always tested. Try again."

"An accidental shooting?"

"Guns aren't allowed in court."

He hunched his shoulders. "Drown him?"

I sighed. "Really Mark; is that all the good you can come up with? You're creativity is lacking," I said, closing my eyes, trying to will my image to return. When I opened them, I was relieved to see myself again in the pane of glass. I wondered if I could restore my *original* looks, but I would have to try another time. Doing these fancy tricks wreaked havoc on my energy.

"Sorry, dear Anne, I'm out of ideas. My talents lean more towards music, dance, and cheerful revelry."

I smiled at him. "No, forgive *me* for being so cross. It's just that I nearly had him right where I wanted him!"

We found out that the guards dragged my latest victim down to the dungeons, and locked her in the stocks for the time being. Since they knew she was like the others, they were going to burn her, and I could not let them. Smeaton and I snuck down there to find her, released her from her bonds, and set her free through a secret passageway that led directly outside. It did not matter to me whether the last of Anthony's victims were found or not. My evil kind were here to stay, and would only grow in number over the centuries.

Once I released her, I had to check on the King and see how he fared after *that* fiasco.

At his door once more, I started to open it, and then remembered what happened to me earlier. If only I could walk through walls!

Smeaton must have read my mind, for he literally poked his head through the wall, listened for a while, then drew his head back out.

Thomas is trying to console Henry right now," he whispered. "The king keeps blubbering about how his 'dear Jane' tried killing him. Thomas is doing his best to convince His Majesty that what he saw was not truly Jane, but an evil demon disguised as her that had to be destroyed. Even so, I don't think he's listening."

"An evil demon that has to be destroyed, hmmm?" I asked, with a hand on my hip.

"Those were his words exactly."

I folded my arms and gave Smeaton a little smirk. "Thomas is going to pay *dearly*," I said to him. "His time is quickly coming to an end."

Chapter Ten

Henry did not know it, but I was allowing him one more night to sleep in his bed before he died. In the meantime, I wanted Smeaton to go and find Thomas, and talk to him. I needed to know exactly what was on Thomas' mind; what made him suddenly decide to do a complete roundabout on me.

Smeaton found him in his chambers, polishing his sword. Thomas had his door opened at a crack, probably listening for intruders -- mainly me. Smeaton brandished a white handkerchief, put his head and his arm through Thomas' wall, and began waving it at him, who took a while to notice. It appeared that he was in deep thought as he cleaned his sword so diligently.

Finally, Thomas glanced up, and saw the small white object flailing about, and the disembodied arm attached to it. Then he saw Smeaton's floating face and his bright smile.

"Truce?" he asked in a meek voice.

"What do you want?" Thomas asked in a flat voice, as dour as usual, tending to his sword again.

"I--I'm just here to talk."

Thomas sighed. "Then speak."

Smeaton stepped all the way into the room, so I tried peeking through the crack in Thomas' door.

"I've been noticing how you and Anne have become... well... *less* than friendly, and I'm merely curious as to what started it all."

Thomas put his sword aside. "Anne has always played games with me, Smeaton, and frankly, I'm finally tired of them. She plays games with my heart, my feelings, and my very being! I never realized she had such a cruel streak in her, and I see it now more than ever, ever since she became that wretched *thing* that she is." His face looked pinched with disgust. "What she did to Charles... how she *treated* him... what she made him do... *that* was the final straw. I do not like what she has turned into. I do not like what she had made of *me*. She was right all along. She and I can never have what we did before. Since she wants to die so much, then I'll *personally* have her meet her maker."

Smeaton looked shocked. "I'm very sorry to hear it, Thomas."

He snorted. "Revenge is a dish best served cold, Mark. Remember that."

I looked away and thought that one over.

It may have been a cold dish, but *I* hadn't finished serving just yet.

***

While they were still conversing, I headed over to Henry's chambers. He wasn't asleep, so I put on my Jane illusion again and entered his room.

He was sitting in a chair by his fireplace, staring into the flames as if in a trance. When he saw me, his eyes widened, and he slowly got up, backing away from me.

"You tried to kill me, Jane!" He looked heartbroken. "Why would you do such a thing? I love you!"

Henry truly was going 'round the twist! "My love, I was angry with grief. I would not have killed you. I miss holding my son. I miss being with you, tending to court with you. There were so many things we could have done together, that we never got the chance to do…"

That eased him immensely. He lowered his guard and approached me.

"Can I… touch you, Jane?"

I closed my eyes for a moment, pretending to be doing something, and then looked at him again. "Now you can, dear husband."

I outstretched my arms, welcoming him with a smile. He walked up to me and wrapped his arms around me.

"Oh, Jane… if this is heaven, I surely do not wish to leave!"

"If only you hadn't let me die…" I said in a dark tone, putting phase two of my illusion to work -- and the pièce de résistance.

He pulled away, no longer seeing Jane's vibrant face, but her decaying one.

Henry kept backing away from me, screaming… screaming… *screaming*!

My appearance was skeletal; a thin layer of dried, brown skin was taut over my skull. My blonde hair was in dirty, drooping strands, my supple skin now a dry husk. I reached my arms out to him, nothing but brown, cracking bones under tattered, filthy, dress sleeves.

"Why did you let me die?" I kept asking, walking slowly towards him. Henry kept shaking his head, eyes round, unable to speak. If I kept this up, he would be as much of a blubbering mess as George made our father.

"God damn you, woman!" Thomas said in the doorway. I turned, dropping my illusion. "I'll not have Edward be without both his parents!"

I hissed at him. This was *it*. I'd *had it* with him!

"How can you have the *gall* to impersonate Edward's dead mother? His Majesty's dead wife? You have no heart, nor a soul!"

"I had no heart once the choice of who I was to love was left to *Fate!*" I spat. "I'm not like *you* Wyatt, whoring around with anything that wears a skirt, trying to fill a void that never can be. You lost your pride, as well as your honor!"

Thomas sneered at me. "Let's take this outside and be done with it," he said, backing away from the door as he faced me. When he was out of my view, he took off, and I chased after him.

I checked court first. It was empty, the hundreds of candles leaving a dull yellow glow throughout the entire hall. I leapt upon a table with catlike grace and scanned the area for any sign of movement.

Thomas knocked over the table I stood on. I fell to the floor hard, then turned and barely got out of Thomas' way as the point of his sword collided with the floor instead of my chest. I kicked at his ankle. He yelled and fell. I grabbed a candelabrum and hurled it at him, hitting him in his face. He yelled again as blood seeped from a scar on his forehead. He got up, and I grabbed a chair next, swung it, and just missed him as he dodged contact with it. The chair crashed against a wall instead, shattering into pieces.

Thomas lunged after me, cutting the air with his sword, missing me by inches. I grabbed a large silver tray from another table, using it as a makeshift shield. He kept attacking, slamming his sword into the tray, dents slowly starting to appear in it. I grabbed another candelabrum, and thrust it at his sword when he came at me again. The blade quickly became wedged in it, so I flung it, both objects hurtling through the air. He became distracted for that one second, so I took the tray and slammed it against Thomas' head. He stumbled backward and shook it off.

"I always knew you'd become a witless ponce," I sneered. "You often complain more than a woman!"

He came right at me, head on. Foolish move.

I grabbed his arms, yanked him towards me to throw him off-balance, and started to spin in place. Once I gained enough momentum, I let Thomas go, sending him sailing across the room, yelling all the way. His body slammed against a wall which housed a stained glass window, colorful shards raining to the floor and tinkling like chimes. I was beginning to *like* that sound.

I looked to the mess. Thomas was unconscious and lying face down. I walked over to him, glass crunching underfoot. I grabbed him by his ankles and dragged him away, tossing his limp body onto another table. I grabbed a decorative staff from another suit of armor, broke it in two with my thigh, and aimed the pointed end at his chest.

"Goodbye... *Thomas Wyatt*," I hissed, thrusting down.

Thomas opened his eyes and cried out in agony, clutching at the staff wedged in his chest. He kicked me away from him and rolled off the table, crawling a few inches before he stopped.

I gave a triumphant laugh.

"Maybe *now* you'll be free of me!" I said loudly to his lifeless body, my voice echoing throughout the room.

Straightening my gown and standing upright, I began to make my way to Henry's chambers, but stopped short when I already saw him standing in the center of court. He looked as if he regained his old self, as if something restored his very will and essence.

"Henry... we meet again," I said with a coy smile.

"I *do not* know you, woman!" he snapped, glaring at me.

"On the contrary, you *do*." I slowly walked towards him, and he raised his sword. "You know me *very* well. We first met at a masquerade ball. If I can recall correctly, my sister -- as well as *your* sister, were part of the festivities as well."

Henry narrowed his eyes, unsure of what to think.

"You even made me one of Katharine's ladies-in-waiting," I continued in a snide voice. "You wanted me, Henry. Oh, how you *wanted* me, and you *always* got what you wanted."

"Enough of this!" he bellowed, getting frustrated.

But I kept going. "Or perhaps mentioning the *Marquess of*

Pembroke will jog your memory?"

Henry frowned. "The Marquess of Pembroke is dead! Quit your foolish lies, stop your pacing, and let me see you!" he said, *still* leery of whom I was!

"And what if I *don't*?" I replied with a smirk, even though he could not see it.

"I am the king, and I *order* you to!"

I sniffed. "Like that matters to me."

"I do not like your tone, woman. I should hold you in contempt."

"Contempt of *what*? And I am not just *some woman*. Like I've said, you know me *very* well."

The next look Henry got on his face was one of sheer disgust, and he narrowed his eyes again as he approached me. Henry and I continued to do a strange, predatory dance around one of the dining tables. His eyes showed nothing but loathing hatred, as if he *might* have known whom I was, but could not *believe* it, and was *praying* it wasn't true. I knew whatever love he had for me was long since gone, but seeing him gaze upon me now would put shivers down *any* woman's spine.

"What manner of darkness has brought you here?" he asked in a low tone, still pointing the sword at me.

"My own foolishness, I'm afraid," I replied. "Foolish thoughts and foolish wishes. And seeing that such thoughts have granted me permission to execute my desires..." I raised my arms. "Here I am, and *have* been -- for over a *year*, now!"

"What *are* you? Some repugnant, foul creature existing only to torment the living?"

"Not everyone -- just *you*." I chuckled. "And those who betrayed me."

He raised his sword. "Reveal yourself, by order of the king!"

I gave him an unrelenting stare, still surprised he did not recognize me from the blatant clues I had given him. Sighing in annoyance, I lowered my hood. He gasped and backed away, still oblivious. I employed my illusion spell once more, showing my original face for a few seconds before it melted away, showing my current one.

His look was a cross between total madness and fury. He pointed at me. "You -- *unholy bitch* from hell! I had you killed! *YOU*! The cause of all my grief and misery, then, *AND* now! With God as my witness, I will surely put you back in hell *myself* -- with my BARE HANDS!"

I laughed at him, and he grimaced in irritation at the sound of it.

"You cannot touch me, Henry. I'd never give you the chance."

"So, you *are* a witch!" He paused, pointing at me again. "They were right about you *all along*. My suspicions were *true*!"

I rested my hands on the top of a chair, trying to control my temper. Unfortunately, the frame of the chair cracked under my grip, and he looked at the chair, then to me again, raising his eyebrow. I was *really* getting tired of hearing those monotonous lines!

"Now see, that's where you are *wrong*, Henry. I think that is your biggest bane. Besides, you and your council were merely looking for something to convict me with then, just so you could have your way with Jane Seymour! It is those same frustrations that have brought me back!"

"How DARE you talk to me that way!"

"I'll talk to you any way I see *fit*!" I snapped. "I *loved* you, and you tossed that to the wind!"

"Your love was nothing but *lies*!"

"As was *yours*! When I was queen, I never betrayed you, *never*! But you listened and *heartily agreed* with the inaccuracies and rumors of your so-called council! If I knew then what I know now, I'd have *gladly* forsaken *everything* to live my life in peace, the way I would have preferred!" I gave him an unyielding stare as I placed my hands on the table. "I want my restitution!"

"The devil's concubine deserves *no* restitution!"

I screamed so loudly, I shook the remaining glass windows until they broke -- tiny, glittering splinters exploding outward, some of them raining down to the floor, clinking against everything while bouncing off of Henry's back. He covered his ears as tiny rivulets of blood seeped between his fingers. He cried out in agony and collapsed to his knees. It gave me the opportunity to reach him, and I bent down, grabbing him by his throat, and squeezed. As I gazed into his eyes, I finally saw the fear in them that I so longed to see.

"You *will* give me my restitution," I repeated slowly. "I will not rest until you do."

Between his gagging and coughing, he managed to speak.

"Bitch of a whore…!"

I balked, surprised at his defiance. Despite his fear, his arrogance prevailed! Perhaps it is true what they say about a king's vaingloriousness!

Still gasping, he watched as I raised a hand to his face, wiggling my pale, thin fingers at him before I touched his cheek. He flinched at their coldness.

"See these clammy hands that touch your skin? My eyes, my face? A spirit that cares not for your pomposity, or your arrogance? You, my father, the Duke, Cromwell… *all* of you have incurred my wrath!"

"Your father failed me! Your whole *family* lied to me!"

I picked him up and threw him. Not giving him a chance to rise, I flew towards him, shrieking, and grabbed him once more, slamming his back against a wall.

"How does it feel to be bullied, Henry? Not so nice, is it?"

He could not answer, so I continued.

"My family was ever obedient to your every whim!" I exclaimed. "And my father served your family well, fighting for *your* father against the Cornish rebels when I was barely conceived!"

For a moment, I received a flash of memory -- my father cowering in a corner, reduced to a blubbering, mentally ill, shell of his former self. Then I remembered spitting on his cold, hard, grave. It was not the father I remembered, and in that moment, I regretted what I had done to him.

Henry saw my moment of falter, and shoved me away. I fell, and Henry grabbed a five-foot tall candelabrum, swinging it at me. I tried getting up, but the candelabra collided with my body, and I fell again. He swung once more, keeping me down on the floor.

"ENOUGH!" I yelled. By sheer force of will, I made the candelabra shoot from his hand, sending it flying across the room. It broke with a metallic clang, a few pieces skidding across the floor.

Henry physically went at me, intending to strangle me to death, but I held out a hand, as if commanding him to stop. His movements now frozen, I shoved him away from me again without touching him. He fell with a thud and cried out in pain. I quickly got up and rushed over to him, looking down at his panicked face.

"I told you I wouldn't give you the chance," I said and grinned. "I'll make you suffer Henry, and suffer *well*. The Boleyns *will* rise to power one day. Too bad you won't be around to see it."

I hunched down and bared my fangs at him. Henry was too paralyzed with shock to do anything. Aiming for his neck, what happened next almost felt as if it happened very slowly, even though it took mere seconds.

Thomas had gotten up, his wound still leaking blood, a trail of it having stained his doublet and breeches. With all the noise of the melee going on, I never noticed he was missing.

I saw his eyes. They locked with mine for a brief moment, and in that moment, I saw the Thomas I knew. The Thomas I had loved. The Thomas that was regretting every second of what he was doing.

"I'm so sorry, Anne," he whispered, a tear running down his cheek "Forgive me."

I saw his sword, and I realized he was *finally* willing to be my savior... as well as his own. A reserve of peace washed over me, and I do believe I even smiled. I thanked God for giving him that strength, that bravery Thomas so desperately needed, and I saw when he swung at my neck, catching a glimpse of the bright glint of the blade as it came towards me, and I remembered nothing else.

Chapter Eleven

A vast amount of time had passed before I became conscious again. Even so, where I materialized was not where I had expected to wind up.

As I was coming to, I found myself immersed in a bright, blinding light. When the light dimmed and faded away, I saw I was in a church. It was unoccupied for the time being, but one can only imagine my confusion. I had expected to remain unconscious forever.

I wandered throughout the church until I came to a tomb. An effigy on top of one of the coffins within bared a beautiful likeness to a woman who obviously was well loved by her people. The other coffin was very ornate, but nothing like the first one I had laid eyes on.

When I approached them, and found out who they were, a hand flew to my chest as I began to hyperventilate.

They were the coffins of *Mary*, Katharine's daughter, and my very own daughter, *Elizabeth*.

How long had I been away?!

At first, I was shocked that they would lay these two *sisters* together. Surely, they had rivaled over the throne...

I ran my hand over the length of Elizabeth's effigy, tears streaming down my face.

"Oh, my Elizabeth," I whispered, leaning over it, pressing my face to the image of her cold, stone one, and closed my eyes. "My dear, sweet child..."

I would have to go to the royal library, and find out exactly what had happened while I was gone.

At Whitehall, there were so many unfamiliar faces. Moreover, from the time span of things, I already knew Henry had long since died. But I did not concern myself with such things. I headed for the library, and looked for a book that recorded the Tudor family history.

Once I was finished, several hours had passed. I also found out Thomas had been very involved in my daughter's life, becoming part of a rebellion against Mary's religious and bloody tyrannies while she was on the throne. I sniffed. Like father, like daughter. Although Thomas' intentions had meant well in wanting Elizabeth to rise to the throne, the way he had recklessly gone about things nearly cost Elizabeth her very life. Sadly, I also found out that Thomas had been beheaded, and drawn and quartered for treason. His head was left on a lance at Tyburn, which eventually had been stolen. I shivered at the thought.

Even so, Elizabeth came out triumphant in the very end, reigning over England for forty-five years, having died when she was nearly seventy years old. England had seen very prosperous, peaceful years in her reign, and knowing that, my heart felt at peace, growing with love and pride for my daughter. *My Elizabeth*. She had done well, and I couldn't have been more proud of her. Although I was a bit surprised that she never married, perhaps it worked out for the better in her case. The follies of men often proved quite troublesome for the fairer sex.

I exited the library and caught my reflection in a window. I gasped, staring at myself in amazement.

I touched my face. I looked like my *normal* self, not that hideous *thing* I had been before! What had I done to earn such a gift? Had I unknowingly performed some strange redemption? Was it an unconscious act of contrition on my part?

Whatever it was, I was glad to be free of that gruesome persona.

I wandered over to a more familiar church next -- the Chapel of St. Peter ad Vincula -- not that I wanted to see the foreboding Tower again. The Chapel seemed to be calling to me, for some odd reason.

It was there that I discovered that I had been given a much more proper burial, and my hands flew to my mouth in surprise. Although there was just a meager stone in the marble floor stating who I was and that I had been the Queen of England, it was still much better than having been tossed in a shallow grave without a marker. I gave thanks to whomever had the decency to do this for me.

It was nearing dusk, and I went back to Whitehall. It was a wonderfully warm summer evening and I wanted to catch the last rays of sunlight before they fell behind the skyline.

I wandered around the ponds in the garden, feeling an insurmountable amount of joy. For some reason, I could not stop smiling. I was *free*.

"It feels good to be able to *genuinely* do that, doesn't it?"

I gasped and turned around, very surprised at who I saw.

"*Thomas?*"

He smiled. I saw the mark of the executioner's axe on his neck, not to mention dark, bruise-like marks around his shoulders.

I embraced him, and a warm glow briefly surrounded us.

"You're looking a lot better," he said jokingly, brushing some of my dark locks away from my face.

"I'm sorry for what happened to you," I said, and looked down.

He understood what I meant. "You've found out the rest of Elizabeth's history since you've returned… and my involvement in it." He gave a half-smirk. "It was for a good cause."

I nodded. "But, why are *you* here?"

"Waiting for *you*, actually," he answered, gesturing across the pond to three more men standing and waiting.

One of them waved his arm high in the air. From the black curly locks on his head, I already knew it was Smeaton. And George! No longer that awful dead thing, but his true, handsome, witty self! The last man was my father, looking a lot more youthful than he had during his last days.

Thomas and I appeared before them, and Smeaton bombarded me with a big embrace.

"My Lady! It's so *good* to see you again! It's been *quite* a while," he said, more happier than usual, then glanced at Thomas. "Couldn't avoid that chopping block, I see." He gave Thomas a funny face as he held his own neck.

Thomas smirked. "Well, at least it was swift."

George chuckled at him, and then looked at me. He touched my face and tilted my chin, getting a good look at me. He simply shook his head and smiled.

"Dear sister," he said, giving me a tight embrace.

"My dear brother," I replied, a tear going down my face.

As they conversed, my father gave me a solemn look, took my hand, and walked off with me for a moment.

"I know I always haven't been a good, loving father," he started. "Call it the flaws of being a soldier." He sniffed, looking down. "I've done things to my family that kept me in remorse long after I left this earth." He took a deep breath, and sat us down on a bench. "How I wanted you to know how much I loved you, and how *very* sorry I was to have taken your joy away from you in your youth. From you *and* your sister. It's only after such precious things have been taken away from you that you realize how priceless they are."

I tried hard not to tremble, as I felt an onslaught of tears coming forth.

He kissed my hand. "My beloved Anne, my daughter, I hope you can forgive me for the wrongs I've done you."

The tears finally escaped me as I embraced my father. Now he was in tears, as well.

"That's all I wanted to hear, father," I whispered. "Thank you."

As we walked back towards George, Thomas, and Mark, I suddenly realized that part of that strange dream I had before was now real. All the gentlemen in my life whom I loved and cared for were here with me right now. All quarrels and disputes had been reconciled. Things were now as they should have been. *Finally*.

I never believed that there would actually be a happy ending for me, but it looked to me that all of our destinies had been fulfilled, and now, we *all* could have our rest.

George put his arm around my shoulder as he spoke to me.

"Our mother and sister are also waiting for us. Mary had been worried about you for so long. She's going to be so happy to see you again! To see you as you are *now*... like you used to be."

I gave a huge grin. "Mother? And Mary, too?" I exclaimed.

George looked over my shoulder, smiled, and then pointed. I turned, seeing my sister running towards me. I laughed, and arms wide, I collided with her, giving her a huge embrace.

"Oh, my dear Anne!" she said happily, holding my face, looking at me. "You're as beautiful as ever!"

I looked over to my mother last, tears in both our eyes. She drew me close to her, stroking my hair.

"My sweet girl," she whispered to me. "Such a hard life you've led, both while alive *and* undead. How I *wished* I could have come to your aid in your darkest hours! No mother likes to see their child suffer, but you've come out of your trials and tribulations on your own terms. No mother can feel as proud as I do."

"I'm just so glad to have *all of you* with me again," I said between sobs. All the riches in the world would not have been more greater than that very moment.

As we took our leave of the world for the last and final time, I could not help but think that Henry's personal horrors and hauntings done by myself were never mentioned in the book, not that I would have expected them to be. They only spoke of his increased illnesses and growing obesity, which caused his own demise.

Nevertheless, despite the omitting of Whitehall's more 'darker' history, one fact would never be forgotten.

I would always remain Anne Boleyn… the first *Tudor Vampire*.

OTHER BOOKS BY THE AUTHOR

Libby Usherick is a modest young lady in her twenties, whose future, hopes and dreams seem lost when her fiancé dies from a horrible illness, leaving her penniless and homeless. It's not until the mysterious Darren Von Trapp--a wealthy, former owner of a popular doll-making emporium--takes Libby under his wing and shows her the love she so yearns for... and a darker, more exciting world underneath the one was so used to, a world she never dreamed she'd take part in. It's a world of decadence, dancing, devilish delights and dark magic, leading to a tragedy she'll be unable to escape--for soon she'll realize, all to late, no matter what happens, the show must go on...

COMING THIS SUMMER, 2010
Check http://BloodTouch.webs.com/TheShow.htm
for details.
Find the trailer: www.youtube.com/cinsearae

SINK YOUR TEETH INTO *THIS* VAMPIRE SERIES...

The ABRAXAS Series: Books 1-3
ISBN: 978-1-4357-2847-9
Available through
www.lulu.com/gratistavampires

Christine Vargas is an independent, young, working class girl, violently swept into another world--a world deemed unrealistic and impossible by many, a world under the mundane one she is so used to. During her physical transition, she has to come to grips with new powers she has been bestowed, and join up with her new 'Lord', Ryan Price, a gentleman of high social status--and twice her age. Her 'new family' is a motley crew of young vampires, and among the family are two rebellious twins trying to dethrone Ryan and take over the clan with their own legion of bloodthirsty (and drug-hungry) vamps. Only Christine can determine the outcome of the oncoming battle and must chose quickly before the unthinkable happens. This is only the start of the strange, twisted, and mystical life Christine is now a part of, as more scarier situations present themselves to her, Ryan, and their delicate ABRAXAS clan---and sometimes, the 'monsters' aren't quite what you'd expect...

Praise for "*The ABRAXAS Series: Books 1-3*"

"I found myself drawn into Ms. Santiago's dark tale. The Abraxas Series offers a different slant on the paranormal; it hits the ground running and keeps the reader enthralled. The characters are well rounded; the story telling will keep you in suspended anticipation. It leaves you wanting more. Highly recommended!" ~**Corvis Nocturnum, Author of "Embracing the Darkness; Understanding Dark Subcultures"** *and* **"Promethean Flame"**

*"These days, the world appears virtually awash in vampire tales, so many of them of-a-piece that sometimes it's hard to remember if you've read the story before! Consequently, it's not just a relief but a true joy to read Cinsearae Santiago's unique **ABRAXAS** series. Her protagonist Christine Vargas is sharp and sassy and tells it like it is, even though she is caught in a world of darkness. Christine is a refreshing no-nonsense character, afraid of neither the living nor the undead, and full of down-to-earth integrity. If you love your vampire fiction full of conflict and romance, I recommend that you give the ABRAXAS books a read."*
~**Nancy Kilpatrick, Author of "The Power of the Blood" series and "The Goth Bible"**

"My first thoughts of this book; absolutely, freaking amazing...This is definitely a book for someone who is in touch with their bad side, and can appreciate the sexy, gothic side to life... If you are someone who is not afraid to read spicy material and allow your blood to heat up, then get cozy and read this book!"
~**FrontStreetReviews.com**

"An engaging and supernatural tale. Exotic and erotic." ~**Mario Acevedo, Author of "The Undead Kama Sutra"**

"Each book builds in intensity until the story explodes off the page and makes you eager for more...Romance is mingled with suspense and creepy situations, making this a gripping read. Sinister and attention grabbing, **The ABRAXAS Series** *will definitely keep you entertained."* ~**Nights and Weekends**

"Ms. Santiago adds a few new twists to the ever popular vampire genre and gives it a unique spin all its own. The way the story ends is a total surprise and very creative if not macabre." **~BittenByBooks.com**

"This is an engrossing and often extremely violent tale...The characters are well written and come to life on the page, and there is a great deal of action throughout the tale, as well as a moving love story." **~Coffee Time Romance**

"Now THIS is what vampires should be all about...Hot, sexy, brash, violent and ghastly...this is the type of vampires I want to read about...the kind that truly scare the crap out of you, make you want to be them...Move over vampires kings, queens and underlings...a new ruler has come to play (take over more like) and her name is Cinsearae Santiago. Realistic and cruel...I had so much fun being "had" by this book. Can't wait to be had again..."
~Andrea Dean Van Scoyoc for Twisted Dreams Magazine

"These stories are smoking hot. You will need an ice cube or a fan to cool down after reading them. The characters are scintillating and you will have a fun time reading all the stories." **~Night Owl Romance**

"Ms. Santiago created a world more interesting than just a typical vampire story that we have all come to know and love...Her characters are amazingly drawn out into this world, where the humans, witches and vampires collide. The plot of the story kept getting thicker and thicker, when you thought they were through with the fighting - you turned the page and you were wrong! Something was always around that dark corner to jump out at you! This was and is going to be on my fave's list!" **~Ruthie's Book Reviews**

"...I absolutely love how descriptive this book is. I actually felt like I was a part of all the action scenes. It was almost as if I was watching a movie rather than reading a book....I enjoyed the love story like any other romance novel, the paranormal flare only added dimensions to it....I can sincerely say that I am looking forward to reading the next book in this series. My attention was definitely intrigued." **~RWA Bookclub**

"Cinsearae Santiago delivers a dark, sexy and bloody tale that will leave most paranormal junkies absolutely hooked. **The ABRAXAS Series** *is loaded with interesting characters that will surprise you at the turn of every page...Ms*

Santiago's writing is original and professional. She presents a well written story that finds a happy medium between fantasy and mysticism. A "must read" for anyone who enjoys fiction that teaches while it entertains."~*The Pagan and the Pen*

"This was most definitely an interesting read, one that was quite hard to put down. Ms. Santiago created such a unique vampire story and obviously has an imagination unlike anyone I have ever known! I do highly recommend the book and look forward to reading the fourth book of the series." ~**Dark Diva Reviews**

ALSO AVAILABLE AT THE AUTHOR'S BOOKSTORE:

ABRAXAS: Seeing Green
Book 4 in the series
ISBN: 978-0-557-07369-6

Edward lies in a coma in the hospital, with Christine having a sneaking suspicion that Ryan has something to do with Edward's current condition. Ryan continues to act strangely possessive of Christine to the point where it becomes too scary for her to deal with. His sexual forwardness doesn't make matters for her easier, either.

Edward's spectral form cries to Christine for help, as the clan soon discovers that Ryan's odd behavior is not his own...and to make matters more trying for her, Christine's best friend stops by for a visit, unknowing of her situation.

AND COMING THIS SUMMER, 2010

ABRAXAS: Judgment
Book 5 in the series

The waters are getting testier when Christine and Ryan have to face the remaining three Elders of their House to assess the progress of their Abraxas Clan, which someone has purported to be too chaotic and disorganized since Christine's arrival.

Magdalene, Kain's mate, passes a special bit of judgment all her own when she offers Christine a 'present' that will test her faith, love and devotion to the Abraxas Clan, as Christine is sent back in time... before she became a vampire.

AND THE FIRST STAND-ALONE NOVELLA FROM THE ABRAXAS SERIES:

ABRAXAS: The Haywire Halloween
ISBN: 978-0-557-06031-3

Abraxas clanster Jonathan stumbles upon a skeleton key he believes was part of someone's Halloween costume. What it really winds up being is a demon's not-so-subtle way of getting Jonathan to do his dirty work for him. Jonathan's wishes start to give his Clan more headache and hassle than the 'fun' he hoped they would, as fellow trick-or-treaters and party goers start becoming the things they're dressed up as---with horrifying results, and much, much worse...

"*...It is a delicious mix of comedy and gore that makes you lick your lips and ask for more.*" **~BittenByBooks.com**

"*OH MY GOD....if you're a Halloween freak, you are in for an ABSOLUTE treat with this novella!*"**~ThePurpleRaven.blogspot.com**

"*THE HAYWIRE HALLOWEEN introduces readers to a plethora of characters and yet each one is distinctive and well developed. The interactions between the characters give a lot of insight into their various personalities and help set the tone for the story. Jonathan's character in particular is one that tugs at the reader's heart. His youthful energy and loyalty to his friends make him endearing even when his fascination with Halloween leads to such disastrous consequences. THE HAYWIRE HALLOWEEN is my first foray into the Abraxas series but it will not be my last as Cinsearae Santiago shows she can weave together one heck of a great tale!"* ---**(5 stars) Debbie Wiley Book Reviews**

ALSO COMING THIS SUMMER, 2010
THE SECOND STAND-ALONE NOVELLA IN THE ABRAXAS SERIES:

Abraxas: Urban Legends

Jonathan's darkly humorous misadventures continue when the gang visits a traveling carnival harboring quite a few dark secrets, involving homunculus-stuffed prizes, zombie groundskeepers, urban legends mysteriously coming to life, and treacherous Carney-folk. When everything's over, Kurt will never let Jonathan live this episode down...

**FIND FREE CHAPTER DOWNLOADS FROM ALL THE ABRAXAS BOOKS, AND VIEW TRAILERS AT:
HTTP://BLOODTOUCH.WEBS.COM/ABRAXAS.HTM**

ABOUT THE AUTHOR

Ms. Santiago is the creator of the all-new, dark paranormal romance series, "**ABRAXAS**". A digital artist, jewelry designer, and still-photographer, Ms. Santiago is also Editor/Publisher of ***Dark Gothic Resurrected Magazine*** -- a top ten finalist in the ***Preditors & Editors Readers Poll for 2008 and 2009*** and winner for "Best Magazine Art"-- having created this publication to give new and unpublished writers and artists of the genres a chance to shine and see their names in print, preferring unique, edgy stories that are out-of-the-box. She also received the ***Author's Site of Excellence Award*** in December 2007 from ***P & E***, and is a Cover Artist for **Damnation Books**. An avid fan of 'old school' horror movies (Freddy, Jason, Michael, Pinhead…) Halloween is her favorite time of the year. She has always been drawn to the flipside of life -- the supernatural, odd, bizarre, Gothic and 'darkly beautiful' always being an inspiration to her.

She can be reached at GratistaVampires@yahoo.com, or http://BloodTouch.webs.com

Made in the USA
Lexington, KY
25 July 2010